Erin Roughley

All the Cats of Cairo

The name of the god who guards you is Cat.

— Spell 145, 12th gate of the "Book of the Dead,"
19th Dynasty (c. 1250 B.C.)

main characters - pink
Settings - blue
Important info. - yellow
~~black~~ Notes - black/~~green~~
word I don't know - blue/pen
Dates - Green

Brown Barn Books
A division of Pictures of Record, Inc.
119 Kettle Creek Road, Weston, Connecticut 06883, U.S.A.

This is a work of fiction; the characters and events to be found in these pages are fictitious. Any resemblance to actual persons, living or dead, is purely coincidental.

Library of Congress Cataloging-in-Publication Data

Schaenen, Inda.
All the cats of Cairo / [Inda Schaenen].—Original paperback ed.
p. cm.
Summary: The daughter of an American diplomat assigned to Cairo, thirteen-year-old Margaret Audrey Underwood is empowered by the ancient cat goddess, Bastet, to help protect her descendants and her people from the plans of a shady American cotton magnate.
ISBN-13: 978-0-9768126-5-4 (alk. paper)
[1. Cats—Fiction. 2. Supernatural—Fiction. 3. Muslims—Fiction. 4. Stuttering—Fiction. 5. Child labor—Fiction. 6. Cairo (Egypt)—Fiction. 7. Egypt—Fiction.] I. Title.

PZ7.S3324All 2007
[Fic]—dc22

2006025613

Printed in the United States of America

*This story is dedicated to Velvet and to the memory of Kyra,
family familiars who helped me appreciate more deeply
the daily life of the cat.*

Acknowledgments

I warmly thank the following readers for their wise, thoughtful, and encouraging feedback on early drafts of this story: Devon Camp, Claire Hentschker, Darcy Camp, Nathan Dee, and Corrie Jolly. Very special loving thanks also to close reader and cat advocate Stella Dee, without whose influence I doubt I would have given much thought to Bastet and her legions.

To Nancy Hammerslough, Kimberly Lake and everyone at Brown Barn Books, I offer thanks galore for their sympathetic support.

And I express profound gratitude to my agent, Laura Dail, who with enthusiasm and perseverance shepherded ALL THE CATS OF CAIRO into the light of day.

She awoke in darkness. Wide green eyes
saw the movement of millions.

Whiskers felt the murmurs of frustration.
Ears heard the cries of the hungry.

And she sensed, with prickly nerves,
that she needed help.

She purred.

At the sound of the purr the earth stirred.

And a young girl heard.

Chapter 1

Signs and Symbols

THE SUN WAS SO BRIGHT Maggie had a hard time gazing at the polished pink spear that rose ninety feet above her upturned face. Not a single cloud marred the perfection of the blue sky. Like the sharpened pencil of a giant, the obelisk pointed straight up. Squinting green eyes against the dazzling light, Maggie tried to decipher the chipped and faded markings carved into each of its four sides.

"I think I see a bird with a p-pointy beak and narrow eyes."

Paul Underwood flipped to the back page of his pocket guide.

"The pointy-beaked bird stands for the letter A."

"So eagle m-means A."

Maggie was mildly disoriented. She wanted the picture of the bird to stand for the bird, not for a boring letter. But as her father explained, twenty different pictures made twenty different sounds. Hieroglyphs could not be more confusing. Sighing, she continued to "read" the obelisk. There was a foot, and a thin sideways rectangle with zigzaggy edges. But the obelisk wasn't telling a story about a person who stepped on a jagged worm; the foot and jagged rectangle spelled *bn*, whatever *bn* meant. It was strange to think that these abstract pictures were actually an alphabet. Then again, everything was strange these days. Ever since stepping off the plane at Cairo International three weeks ago, the *not-strange* moments were the ones that stood out. Luckily, Margaret Audrey Underwood liked strangeness.

After three weeks of the constant crowding and noise of Cairo, she appreciated an outdoor experience that didn't involve pushing, shoving and breathing the mingled smells of cooking oil, cumin, piled up garbage, and overheated human bodies. Before the family left Washington, Maggie's parents had warned her about culture shock, but she'd brushed off these warnings just as, years ago, she'd brushed off reminders to look both ways when crossing the street. She knew life in Cairo would be different from her regular life; she just hadn't imagined how different. Sure, she was an ocean away from her friends, but daily e-mails to and from Cairo had easily taken the place of I.M.-ing at home. She had a pretty good idea of who was liking whom, and who was frustrated with which teacher. And anyway, it was only a year. She'd be going back at the end of next summer. In a way, Maggie was relieved to have a break from the social whirl of eighth grade. It was other things that felt weird.

At home, for one thing, SUVs and minivans swirled on the streets taking people from place to place—work and school and the mall and soccer practice and piano lessons. Here cars jammed the roads too, but they were tiny and tinny, and spewed thick smoke into the faces of people on foot. Everywhere and all the time, Maggie felt like she was crowded out of her own space by other people. People with their voices and smells, their opinions and gestures. Old people and young people hanging out on corners or leaning out of windows to watch the action on the street. At all times of day, Cairo was like a bustling, packed school hall between periods. Seventeen million people. A million spewing cars.

But not right now. Now she was practically alone with this enormous stone from the ancient past.

"There's an owl," Maggie said. "W-what letter is 'owl.'?"

"Owl, owl... Owl is 'M.'"

"And what about that cute little b-bird with the smallish beak?"

"Let's see...That quail stands for either U, V, or W, depending on the word."

Maggie stared at the obelisk, puzzling over the signs left by stonecutters thousands of years ago. It was Maggie's way to think things through in silence. Fear of hearing herself stammer, and a dread of watching another person's face as she struggled to get the sound out, often kept her from sharing thoughts aloud.

"Dad!"

"What?"

"Could those three b-birds in a row—the owl, the eagle, and the cute little quail—see them? About halfway up but a little closer to the top? Could they spell *m-mau*?"

"I suppose so. Why?"

"Because," Maggie replied, her face beaming at the discovery. "Those are m-my initials."

"Cool."

Maggie saw that her father wasn't nearly as intrigued as she was. He was scraping a pebble loose from the tread of his running shoe.

"I wonder what *m-mau* means in ancient Egyptian," Maggie said. "I hope something good."

At least the morning was turning out all right. Following the long, smelly ride in the rattling Metro, a street urchin in rags had offered to trade a broken water pipe for her backpack. Maggie wanted to make the trade—she thought water pipes were cool—but her father had said no. Paul shooed away the disappointed boy. Maggie had been annoyed and wished she could have been by herself. On her own, she would have made the trade. It was so exasperating always having to be with one of her parents. They assured her that at some point she'd be able to move around Cairo with a little more independence, but so far they kept saying no. It was still too new for all of them, they said.

But that was this morning. Now that she was staring at an actual obelisk in peace and quiet, Maggie's irritability was gone.

Maggie reached up to cinch her ponytail tighter. The carved wooden clasp she'd bought at the outdoor market on her second day in Cairo just didn't hold her hair as tightly as the ties she got by the dozen at Wal-Mart. Strands of her light brown hair kept slipping out.

Her eyes slit against the violent sun, Maggie tried to absorb the meaning of the ancient artifact. She continued to wonder about the meaning of *MAU*.

"P-please pass me the book, Dad."

Maggie paraphrased from the guide. "The Egyptians called this p-place On. The Greeks called it Heliopolis, the City of the Sun. Either way, it's described like a kind of Garden of Eden. According to the m-myths, it's where something emerged from n-nothing." She paused and turned to her father.

"How old d-did you say this obelisk is?"

"Let's see." Paul grabbed the guidebook and turned to the page he'd dog-eared last night in bed. "It was built in 1940 B.C."

Maggie thought for a minute. Almost four thousand years ago.

Maggie had a weird feeling in the pit of her stomach. The obelisk was so immense, so permanent. It seemed so different from real life. Everything in real life was always changing. Her favorite TV show. Her favorite sport. Her favorite ice cream flavor. How she wore her hair. The very shape of her body. Nothing about her stayed the same from year to year. Stuff outside herself, too. Neighborhood shops, the movie and music posters on the walls of her friends' bedrooms. Sometimes the friendships themselves shifted. One day someone was your best friend, the next day they refused to sit with you at lunch. And she'd seen more than one of her friends go from ecstatic to miserable in a single period. Even James, the boy who liked her all last year, had e-mailed Maggie that he found it too hard to "keep up their relationship from so far away" and was now going out with Amy Moldawi.

Not that change was a problem. Maggie knew that change could be a good thing. Maybe the problem was sudden, drastic change, which was always scary. Somehow, transformations were easier to deal with when they happened slowly over time, kind of like evolution.

But maybe instant change wasn't the scary thing either. Maybe the scary thing was when things that changed all the time, like people, were right next to things that hardly ever changed for thousands of years, like this stone. Maybe that's what made her feel unsettled. Her always-changing self standing next to a giant rock that hadn't changed in four thousand years.

They turned away from the obelisk to search for a shady place to sit and order a glass of *shay naana,* cold tea with fresh mint leaves. This was Maggie's favorite drink in Egypt so far. But it was late morning and the sun's glare made it hard to see. Paul used his hand as a visor and surveyed the area; Maggie turned back to the shaft of pink granite.

"Dad! L-look!"

"What?"

"Over there, r-right at the base of the obelisk."

"What is it? I don't see anything."

"It's a cat. See?"

"Where, exactly?"

Maggie raised her arm and pointed directly at the creature that was lying peacefully beside the square blocky base. The cat had a beautiful tawny coat of yellow and gold stripes. Its eyes were slitted small against the flood of sunlight. One foreleg lay gracefully across the other, paw resting on paw like a picture Maggie had once seen of Queen Victoria with her thick hands at rest in her lap.

"I see it," Paul said.

"Dad, that cat was not there a m-minute ago. Where did it come from?"

"It must have walked up while we were looking the other way."

"No way! I only looked away for a s-second."

"Maggie, let it go," Paul said, still looking for a suitable place to rest. "It's no big deal."

"I guess… It's an awfully pretty cat though. It sort of l-l-l, has the same look as Sarah."

Sarah was Maggie's cat, a middle-aged, bottom-heavy tortoise-shell who liked to sit on the windowsill and watch pigeons and squirrels. From her first days in the family as a kitten, Sarah galumphed up and down the halls in a heavy-footed hurry. Nobody in the family was ever taken by surprise by Sarah's presence; she did not tread on silent cat's paws. In other ways, too, Sarah was unlike other cats. People think of cats as clean animals, but Sarah always made a mess when she ate. At mealtimes, her smacking and gulping scattered brown kibble all around the base of her food bowl. Also, Sarah tended to ravage carbohydrates. Maggie loved watching her feast on leftover pancakes and rip into bags of sandwich bread. In minutes, Sarah could tear a whole loaf to bits with her teeth and claws. And Maggie had spent many toothbrushings watching Sarah shred and scatter unprotected rolls of toilet paper across the bathroom floor. This drove Maggie's mother crazy. But Maggie adored Sarah, and Sarah slept every night on Maggie's bed, sometimes even tucked under the covers. On hot nights she stretched lengthwise on the cool surface of Maggie's desk. It had been harder to say goodbye to Sarah than to her friends. Her parents assured her that Sarah would be happy with the neighbors; Maggie wasn't so sure.

Maggie followed her father away from the obelisk toward a low curb in the shade of an overhanging balcony. When she turned back one last time, the golden cat opened its eyes wide and looked her straight in the eye. Then it spoke.

"M-m-mraugh...m-m—mraugh."

To Maggie's ears, the cat's call sounded an awful lot like *MAU. And it even seemed to stammer over the M.*

She answered back. "M-m-m-mau."

The cat approached.

Chapter 2

First Things First

Maggie felt the golden cat rubbing against her legs. It closed its eyes and purred. Maggie watched, speechless. She looked around for someone who might be the cat's owner, but the only person nearby was an old bearded man at a café table a few feet away. It was hard to see him from where she stood because his table was in deep shade under an awning, Maggie shielded her eyes to get a closer look. He didn't seem aware of the cat at all. He was just sitting in a bentwood chair reading a newspaper. He wore a roomy black jacket and had a red fez on his head, the kind of tasseled felt hat Maggie recognized from illustrations of Middle Eastern fairy tales. The old man wore white socks and black leather slippers.

"D-dad, let's go sit down over there. I'm boiling."

Maggie and Paul sat down at a free table and the golden cat lay down across her sandaled feet. The warm fur was soft between her toes; the thrumming hum of its purr tickled her skin. Afraid her dad might shoo it away, Maggie kept her legs still and didn't look down. She drank from her bottled water and took a closer look at the old man at the next table. He had dark hairs in his ears and nose. Just then he cleared his throat and spat. Maggie was still getting used to public spitting.

"I don't see any t-t-t...other tourists at all here."

Across the square and into the distance, crisscrossing banners of colorful laundry waved in the shimmering heat. The lines stretched from window to window as far as Maggie could see, connecting the raw red brick houses in a web of cloth.

"We'll have to come back when your mom gets a break," Paul said, putting the water away. "But these first weeks are going to be intense for her. A newly arrived embassy attaché has a lot to learn in a short time."

"Yeah. We're like the attachés of the attaché. We b-brief her on the stuff she doesn't get to do."

Paul laughed and gave his daughter's hand a squeeze. "Exactly. Lucky us. So you want to hear the story of this place, Heliopolis slash On?"

"Sure."

As Paul began, Maggie noticed a second cat, a black and white one with large ears, silently arrive and lie down in the shade near her chair. Hearing yet another meow, Maggie turned and saw a third cat—a velvety, all-black shorthair—under the chair of the man reading the newspaper. The black cat watched her from behind his legs. Maggie stared back at it but said nothing. Paul glanced at the cats gathering around.

"Maybe they're used to people giving away food," he said.

"I guess. I wish I had something to f-feed them. There sure are a lot of c-cats around here. It's a little weird."

Maggie was beginning to feel uneasy. She tried to shift her feet out from under the golden cat but it didn't budge.

"Well, anyway," Paul began, "once upon a time in the beginning of time there was nothing in the world at all. Nothing but ooze, I should say. No cities, no life forms, no bodies of water. Nada. Not even a Starbucks."

Maggie feigned a gasp of shock. Her father nodded solemnly and continued.

"Suddenly, here in this place, right where we're sitting, a mound formed out of the ooze. The mound was called Benben. Out of this mound rose the sun. The sun took the form of a god called Atum. The glowing sun that was Atum rose out of the mound, which is usually drawn as a pyramid. From the top of the pyramid, or Benben, Atum lit up the whole world. Eventually Atum gave birth to two more gods—Shu and Tefnut—who flew out of his nose and mouth.

"Shu and Tefnut, as they say in the Old Testament, begat Geb and Nut, who begat the rest of the nine principal gods of On: Osiris, Isis, Nephthys, and Seth. When Atum saw all he had created, he burst into tears. Can you guess what the tears became?"

"Umm....fish? Grass? No wait, I'll think of it. Give me a s-sec."

The black and white cat trilled a small sound. A fly was crawling along in the dust just out of reach.

"Human beings!"

"Bingo. We are the tears of Atum. Now check this out."

Paul unzipped his beat-up backpack and pulled out his hard-covered sketchbook. Tucked between pages like a bookmark was a dollar bill. He pulled out the bill and handed it to Maggie. The golden cat flicked its tail against her leg.

"What do you see?"

"I see George W-washington."

"Flip it over, Maggie."

Maggie turned over the bill to look at the back side, the lighter side. In a circle on the left side of the bill, next to the word "One," was the image of a pyramid. The topmost point of the structure was severed from its base and surrounded by a glowing triangle that radiated light. Within this triangle was an eye.

"Is that s-supposed to be Benben with Atum on t-top?"

"It is."

"Cool!"

"I think the idea was to link the birth of the new nation, the United States of America, with the birth of the world itself, at least, with the Egyptian version. Pretty nifty, if you ask me."

Maggie twirled her ponytail and thought for a moment. The cats tapped their tails and blinked yellow eyes in the morning heat. Sometimes her dad's stories were annoying, but Maggie thought this one was pretty interesting. It was one of those moments when she was glad her father was an art teacher. He noticed things other kids' fathers didn't. Who else paid attention to the pictures on a dollar bill? And it *was* a little amazing that something as everyday as a dollar bill had so much to do with Egypt, of all places.

The quiet was disrupted by a loud, electric sound—sort of like a song—that seemed to come from a loudspeaker not far away. It was the *zuhr*, the noon call to prayer. Five times a day every single day, all over Cairo, amplified chants invited observant Muslims to their sanctuaries. Behind her, the man in the bentwood chair folded up his newspaper and shuffled off. As he passed, Paul looked up into the brown weathered face and smiled.

"Good morning, sir. You have a city of treasures here."

"Al-hamdu lil'llah," the old man replied. "Praise be to God! Thank you for your gracious words."

Maggie stood up and watched as other men appeared from the shadows of the alleys and low cement government buildings. Everyone hurried toward the golden-hued mosque across the square. Above the rooftops, she saw a skyscape of spindly minarets and domes that reminded her of upended onion bulbs.

As it had for thousands of years before Islam came to Egypt, the obelisk stood erect amid the commotion. As Maggie's eyes drifted toward its point, she could have sworn she saw it vibrate.

The three cats scattered into the shadows.

Chapter 3

Diplomacy

TUCKED IN A CORNER OF her mother's office later that day, Maggie sat in silence. She was steaming mad and exhausted. All she had wanted to do was go home, but her father wanted another hour on the street—alone. He had reminded her, somewhat sternly, that it was important that he spend enough time sketching each day in order to compile the images for a social studies textbook he had been contracted to illustrate. That's why he was taking the year off from teaching, so the whole family would be able to enjoy this year in Cairo together. If he had not arranged for this sabbatical, Paul said, Maggie's mother would have spent the year alone. Maggie understood, but was no less peeved. After a long day on the streets, Paul had dropped her off at her mom's office. Here she would hang out until her mom was ready to bring her home. Just like a little kid. Maggie fumed. This bare office reeked of cigarette smoke and cleaning fluid. It was the last place she wanted to be. How long would this stupid meeting with this Egyptian guy take anyway?

The street racket from outside poured in through a dirty half-open window.

"Hang on a second, Excellency, I'm going to close this window so we can hear each other better."

Maggie's mother, Elizabeth McKee, was a sturdily built, compact woman, the opposite of her long-limbed daughter and lanky husband. Neatly dressed in a simple navy blue business suit and plain pumps, she went to the window and tried to lower it.

Maggie listened to the sounds of the street as her mom struggled with the sticky window. In Cairo there were always horns honking and people shouting. Thanks to all the walking Maggie had been doing, she could picture the variety of vendors yelling for customers—outdoor merchants who hawked carpets, tee shirts, jewelry, electronics, and trinkets; and the people of the food stalls who offered melons, dates, and snacks of steaming, slow-cooked fava beans. Young children were always squealing in frantic games of hide-and-seek and tag. Over the human voices, bus engines ground through gears, dogs barked, and donkeys brayed. It was round-the-clock rowdiness.

Every so often angry voices erupted through the general din, one furious man spitting out Arabic curses against another. Within minutes, a bunch of other voices interrupted the argument and the fight died down. Maggie knew all about these brawls. The first time she witnessed one she had been terrified. But then she learned how they happened. Because Cairenes lived so tightly packed in their city, street fights were common. Neutral onlookers made it a point to break up the face-offs that came about because of sheer crowding. It was a kind of ritual release. Even if things seemed chaotic,

Maggie learned that there was usually a rhyme and reason to life on the street.

Her mother continued to struggle with the unbudgeable window.

"Please, Madame McKee, allow me. And I invite you to call me Shawqi."

"Gladly, Shawqi," said Elizabeth, backing away from the window and returning to her desk. "If you'll call me Elizabeth. You know, I'm still having trouble adjusting to the noise. I feel like I ought to be able to block it out, but I can't seem to."

Shawqi Mahfouz shrugged sympathetically. A native Cairene and an official in the Ministry of Foreign Trade, he was accustomed to watching foreign diplomats come to terms with the realities of his city. The tidy, organized ones had the hardest time.

"Even apart from the noise, it isn't easy for a woman to hold her own in the male-centered affairs of Egypt," the minister said. "You must be very good at what you do." He turned to Maggie. "And you must be very proud of your mother."

Maggie smiled a thin smile. She was used to people saying this. "Y-yes."

Now it was Elizabeth's turn to shrug. "You know, Shawqi, we American mothers who work often suspect that our daughters would rather have us home baking cookies."

Maggie wondered if this was true for her. If her mother had stayed home, she'd never be in Egypt. After-school cookies or Egypt. Not a hard choice. Suddenly she felt a little less mad. Maybe it wasn't so bad to be a fly on the wall. She looked at her mother, who winked at her.

Finally the window was shut as tightly as possible: no fresh air, no sunshine, no street racket.

Poised and elegant in a simple metal folding chair, the minister crossed his legs.

"As you know, Elizabeth, we are trying very hard to encourage international investment in our country. Oil and tourism alone cannot feed, clothe, and house our people. This country is still trying to open up its economy from the days when we tried our hand at socialism. But there are problems. We are experiencing a population growth that overwhelms our ability to provide basic services—housing, electricity, water, road repair, and sewer lines. The things you Americans take for granted. We have a radical religious element that is suspicious of the western influences we cultivate in order to pull ourselves into the 21st century. A third of our people are children. Children! I do not exaggerate. People under fifteen years old. Younger than this young lady sitting right here."

Maggie shifted uncomfortably as the adults glanced at her briefly. She didn't like being brought into the conversation. And she didn't understand what difference it could make to Egypt that there were so many kids in the population. She thought it would be cool if a third of the people in the U.S. were kids. Maggie had just turned thirteen in June.

"Of these," the minister continued, "nearly 300,000 of them in Cairo alone are working in what you would call sweatshops just to help their families survive."

The minister shook his head. After a pause, he pulled out a gold and mother-of-pearl cigarette case. He wordlessly offered a cigarette to Elizabeth. When she declined, he lit one for himself with a silver lighter.

Sweatshops! Maggie wondered why her mother didn't respond to that fact. Kids slaving away in sweatshops was a pretty bad thing. She had read something about sweatshops in a *Time For Kids* back in fifth grade. The one she read about made sneakers, she thought. Or maybe tank tops. Maggie couldn't really remember anything except the pictures that went with the story. The serious faces of all those kids her age bent over machines.

Maybe her mother didn't know what to say. Maybe, Maggie suddenly thought, her mother had a reason for letting the unpleasant fact hang in the air. The Egyptian continued.

"As hard as it is for our traditionalist politicians and fundamentalist religious leaders to accept, we must take the plunge. But we cannot proceed without western resources. I have been approached by an American businessman about buying into one of our premium cotton facilities in Zagazig."

"I know," Elizabeth said. "Mr. Ramsey has already registered his intentions with us here at the embassy. This is strictly protocol. Because of the delicate nature of U.S. relations with the Muslim world right now, our State and Commerce Department guidelines suggest that any business contacts be cleared through the embassies."

"Of course, of course," said Minister Mahfouz. "What I want to know, Elizabeth, is whether you are giving your blessing to Mr. Ramsey's plan. Is your government in support of Egypt's reaching out for financial help or are you here to keep him from proceeding?"

Maggie struggled to follow the conversation. She wondered what her mother would say. She knew her parents' politics were considered liberal—they often joked about being aging hippies—but she also knew that even her mother and father sometimes argued about the best way to accomplish certain goals. Paul usually wanted Elizabeth to be more outspoken about the causes that mattered to them. Elizabeth would reply that a person in her position had to take a more guarded approach. Maggie wondered again why her mother did not simply say that she was all for economic development as long as sweatshops have nothing to do with the business.

In the silence, Maggie studied the Egyptian. His dark hair was combed back over his high forehead and held in place with a shiny gloss of paste. His tan business suit and soft Italian loafers showed her that he was a man who took appearances seriously. Could someone so polished approve of her frumpy mom?

"Shawqi, I have been assigned here specifically to shepherd Mr. Ramsey's project through to a successful conclusion. Successful for him as a representative of the United States textile industry, and successful for our Egyptian associates in Zagazig. Just so you know, I answer directly to Henry Baumsdorfer, the community and corporate affairs liaison who in turn reports directly to our ambassador. As a rule, our government tends to believe that normalization of relations is more, not less, possible when two countries have business interests in common. I understand Mr. Ramsey is meeting today with a Mr.—"

Elizabeth shuffled through a file on her desk.

"Moussa," said the minister. "Farouk Moussa. Yes. Mr. Ramsey and Mr. Moussa are walking through the mill this afternoon. The al-Nasr Qalawun facility in Zagazig is quite productive but already operating at maximum capacity. Spinning, weaving, knitting, and finishing are all managed on site. With the highest quality raw material and a cheap pool of labor at our disposal, the plant is poised for significant growth. The environs of Zagazig are prime for development. Should Mr. Ramsey be so inclined," Minister Mahfouz added with a smile.

"How far away is Zagazig?"

"About an hour and a half by train. Less than half that by auto."

"I suppose he'll be too tired to meet over dinner tonight to discuss his observations," Elizabeth said. "Why don't I give you a call to arrange a time when we can all three sit down together."

"I think it would be a good idea if the plant's director of operations could be at this meeting as well," the minister said, mashing his cigarette into an unused glass ashtray on Elizabeth's desk.

Minister Mahfouz exhaled a long stream of blue smoke. The louvered door to Elizabeth's office opened and a tall, straight-backed man entered. His skin was dark and smooth; his smile revealed straight white teeth. The man wore a red and silver pillbox cap and a traditional red shirtdress over loose green trousers. Over the shirt he wore a red and green vest stitched together with silver threads. From the bottom cuff of his trousers a pair of black Reeboks stuck out like snouts.

"Excuse me, sir," the man said to the minister. "It is time for us to be setting off for your engagement in Heliopolis."

"Elizabeth, please allow me to introduce my driver, Nazaret. Nazaret, this is Elizabeth McKee. I am sure, Elizabeth, that you will one day soon have the opportunity of experiencing firsthand the stellar navigational skills of this man, an Egyptian of proud Nubian lineage."

Nazaret laughed at the high-flown introduction. Elizabeth stood up to clasp Nazaret's hand. They exchanged a firm shake. Nazaret dipped his head to all the adults and turned to Maggie.

"And this is my daughter, Margaret. Margaret Audrey Underwood."

Maggie stood and shook the large warm hand.

"Maggie," Elizabeth said. "Weren't you and your dad in Heliopolis this morning?"

"Uh, yeah!"

"I doubt it's the same place," the minister said. "They probably went to the site of ancient Heliopolis, On, the place the Greeks called the City of the Sun. I'm afraid we are heading for a much younger neighborhood. Our new Heliopolis is a luxury garden suburb developed a hundred years ago by a Belgian businessman. You see," the minister joked, "we Egyptians are no strangers to foreign investors. You might say, and I'm sure Nazaret here would agree, that our population would be nothing but simple Nile valley farmers were it not for foreign trade and investment. Greeks, Romans, Persians, Ottomans, Europeans, Africans—for thousands of years the whole world has laid claim to Egypt and her people."

Nazaret nodded, laughed silently, and looked down.

"But I am impressed to hear about the excursion of your intrepid husband and this young American," the minister said, rising to leave. "Not many visitors take the trouble to board a train and head out to an industrial wasteland that has nothing to show for itself but an obelisk and a bunch of tumble down blocks of stone."

"Oh, my husband likes to get off the beaten path. He says that's what sabbaticals are *for*. And Maggie here is game for anything."

Maggie wished her mother wouldn't make her sound so nerdy—*game for anything*—ugh!

"With a mother in your position, Elizabeth, I am not surprised to hear this. And it sounds like your husband has a feel for travel, too. Perhaps I shall have the honor of meeting him one day."

"No doubt you will, Shawqi. Paul must get some work of his own done during this year, but I am sure he will join us for certain functions."

The Egyptians left. Elizabeth came over to Maggie and swept a strand of hair out of her eyes.

"Sorry for embarrassing you."

Maggie shrugged. She felt crabby, dirty, and exhausted. One second her mother drove her crazy, the next second she felt proud, lucky, and amazed at where she had ended up just by being born to the two people who happened to be her parents. The telephone rang shrilly. Her mother spoke into the intercom.

"Yes?"

"A Bill Ramsey on the line."

"Thank you. You can put him through."

"Well, I just wanted to check in with y'all like a good boy," a loud voice said. From across the room Maggie could hear it easily. Her mom was holding the receiver about six inches away from her ear.

"Mr. Ramsey? This is Elizabeth—."

"—McKee, the lady wearin' the pants around here. Some functionary over at the main embassy transferred me to y'all's office, and I wanted to report that I have finished my meeting up here in North Bejeesus, Egypt. Everything went fine as wine with Moussa, and I am headin' back to my hotel because I am swelterin', just swelterin'. No wonder the weevils leave these here fields alone. They're too damn hot. We didn't see everything, but I'm goin' back there on Monday morning to speak with the chief construction engineer on the project. Please consider this your heads up for that little adventure."

"I'm glad things went well, Mr. Ramsey," Elizabeth said. "Please know that you are invited to be our guest at an embassy party Saturday night—the day after tomorrow—over at the Egyptian Museum. I hope we will see you there."

"Got it, ma'am. It's on my little ol' BlackBerry, which in this heat is liable to bake itself into a cobbler. You will surely see me there. I look forward to toasting the good health of our little enterprise."

Elizabeth hung up and shook her head once each way as if to get water out of her middle ear.

"Could that Ramsey be any worse?"

"Who's Ramsey and w-what's wrong with him?" Maggie asked.

"He's what people call a cock-sure American," her mother said. "And I'm too spent to explain what's wrong with him right now. Let's beat it."

It was close to six o'clock when Elizabeth and Maggie set off for home. A short Metro ride brought them to the general area of the family's rented flat. Once in the neighborhood Maggie asked if they could take a roundabout route from the Metro station. Every day Maggie learned something new about the twisty streets between the Citadel, where the Metro let out, and the Khan al-Khalili market, which was near her apartment.

Nearing home, Maggie saw an older woman sitting on a turquoise piece of cloth spread on a stone front stoop. She wore dirty, well-worn sandals that criss-crossed over her feet. Her head was covered by a navy blue *hijab* patterned with large red flowers. The scarf seemed cheerful compared to her black sack of a dress. A gold bangle gleamed against her yellowish brown skin. The long convex arch of her nose was an inch away from a magazine, on which she concentrated intently. Next to the steps stood a stack of wooden cages filled with live chickens and white pigeons. And next to the bottom cage lay a calico cat with pale green eyes oblivious to the chirping and cooing going on behind its back. Maggie looked at the cat. It got up and meowed at her.

"*MAU.*"

Maggie was a little startled to hear this cat meow the same syllable as had the golden cat from the obelisk. She tried to echo the sound.

"Meow."

The cat lifted its tail higher and shut its eyes. It approached Maggie and rubbed against her legs. She felt a keen vibration at the contact, almost like a small electric shock. Then the calico cat turned away and strolled back to the cage of fowl. Maggie watched it lie down along the wooden frame. Her eyes fell upon a black and white hen inside the cage.

"Mom, can we bring a chicken home for d-dinner?"

"If you're willing to wring its neck, sure."

"Uh, m-maybe not then."

Maggie and Elizabeth turned to go. They stopped at a produce stand and bought a cantaloupe and four slightly bruised yellow apples. A few yards down the street Maggie jostled into position at a fish stall, but before they could order, the buzzing call to sunset prayers crackled over a nearby loudspeaker and jump-started the street into a fever pitch of excitement and movement. An old woman bumped against Maggie's side and muttered what Maggie assumed was an apology. The chanting chorus of *muezzins*, the people who called the men to the mosque, could be heard from every direction. Maggie and Elizabeth decided to pick up the fish closer to home.

Just outside their building they bumped into Paul. The family was renting a two-bedroom flat that belonged to a history professor on sabbatical from the American University in Cairo. Most Americans living in Cairo stuck to the area called Maadi where the shops, restaurants, and schools felt more familiar. But Maggie's father had said he really wanted to live Cairene life, not suburban life transplanted to northeast Africa. What was the point of a year abroad if you surrounded yourself with other Americans? Elizabeth and Maggie agreed. So here they were in the neighborhood known as Islamic Cairo. So far, they were happy. Once in a while someone in the family craved a bagel or a cup of coffee in a place where women and men could chat freely in English. Then they'd make it a point to go where the other expatriates were.

The apartment was comfortable but not roomy. Accustomed to the huge Georgetown townhouses and suburban colonials of her friends, Maggie loved the coziness of the flat. She was relieved to finally get home after a long day tromping about.

"I think living here is going to help me s-stop biting my nails."

"What do you mean?"

"Look at my hands. They're incredibly ashy and s-sandy. If I even so much as raise one finger to my m-mouth, the thought of what could be on them makes me stop dead."

Elizabeth laughed.

"I may even need to borrow your nail clippers. When was the last time I actually cut my fingernails?"

"Can't say I remember."

"Maybe I could grow them out here. I've always wanted f-fabulous claws."

She raised her hands as if to paw at her mother.

"Now, now. You know scratching's not ladylike, Maggie."

"When have I ever b-been ladylike?"

"Good point."

In the cool emptiness of the lobby, Paul pulled out his keys to unlock the front door. As he turned the handle, Maggie heard a faint sound coming from the rear hall where the postman delivered the mail into individually labeled slots. She turned and strained her eyes and ears. It was a cat. For sure it was a cat.

"M-mom!" Maggie whispered as loudly as she could. "M-mom! Come here!"

Her parents had already disappeared inside the apartment. Maggie considered running to drag one of them out, but then—as if pushed along by an outside influence—she turned away from the apartment door and headed slowly toward the mailboxes.

A large cat was lying at the bottom of a brown corrugated box. The top flaps of the box were shredded and bent. Snuggled around the mother slept kittens that couldn't have been more than six weeks old. The mother cat looked up at Maggie with slit eyes. A faint growl rumbled in her throat.

Maggie made herself move as slowly and as quietly as she could. She crouched down and uttered soothing sounds. On the side of the box she saw the Nike logo.

"It's okay. I'm not going to hurt you or your f-family. You're about the f-fiftieth cat I've seen today."

The mother cat's growl grew a little louder, but she opened her eyes fully at the human. Maggie looked right back at her. The mother was lying on her side. Even in the darkness of the hall Maggie could distinguish the two tones of her coat: dark gray stripes on a pale gray background. The cat had a pinkish nose and paw pads to match. Maggie saw dark stripes on the cat's forehead, the same wishbone pattern Sarah had on her caramel and black fur. Often Maggie traced her finger along these wishbone lines of Sarah's fur.

Maggie tried to determine how many kittens the mother cat was nursing. From above they had looked like a big heap of fur; up close she counted limbs, tails, and paws. One kitten was gray like its mother. Another was ginger and tan with a white belly. The third was all white. Six little pointy ears were buried in their mother's fur.

Maggie was so busy taking inventory she didn't even notice when the mother cat stopped growling. Nor did she notice the precise moment when, in that curious way that cats have, the outside curve of her mouth curled into a smile.

Chapter 4

A World in the Cracks

"Listen," Maggie said quietly to the gray cat. "I bet you could use a little extra f-food around here. I'll go in and find something you'll like."

She paused before leaving, wanting so much to reach out and scratch behind the mother's ears. But she knew she shouldn't. Not yet, anyway. She told herself to be patient.

Inside the apartment Elizabeth was chopping onions and cabbage. Waiting for dinner, Maggie thought about the cat at the obelisk in Heliopolis that morning. And the cats by the old man in the shade. And the calico cat in the market place next to the wooden bird coop where that old woman with the bangle bracelet had been reading her magazine so intently. Everywhere she went in Egypt she saw cats. They were everywhere, as common as cars and garbage and scraggly kids. Kind of like pigeons in Washington. But cats were so much nicer to have around than pigeons. Pigeons were dirty, flappy, and annoying, more flying rodent than bird. Cats were pets. Stray cats seemed to be the pets of this whole country. Some looked scruffy and lean, others sleek and regal. Strange. Maggie wondered what Sarah would make of this. How would a pampered and idiosyncratic American house cat fit in here? Especially one who attacked loaves of bread and rolls of toilet paper for no apparent reason.

It was too early to ask to keep one of the kittens. Much too early. She'd start with just a little private care, off the premises, and see where that would lead. After all, she *had* tried to catch her mom's attention. It wasn't as if she were doing anything sneaky.

"Hi, sweetie," Elizabeth said. "Dad's in the tub. Use the kitchen sink for your hands."

"Okay. What are you making?"

"Potatoes and vegetables with a sort of minty yogurt sauce like the one we had in that restaurant the other night. I'm trying to replicate it on my own. And I'll fry the fish we just got, too."

Maggie had been craving a bath, but with her father in the bathroom and her mom preoccupied with dinner, now was a perfect time to deliver a meal to the cats in the hall.

Maggie bent down to the small refrigerator and found the fish package wrapped in that day's issue of *Al-Akhbar,* the racy daily newspaper read by those with a taste for crime and gossip. In the package were three scaly river perch her mom was going to make for dinner. Beside the perch lay five or six tiny crustaceans that the vendor had thrown in for free when she noticed Maggie staring at them. Maggie tore off a corner of the paper and scooped them up.

It was easy enough for Maggie to slip out the door and return to the cat family. The kittens were still snuggled up against their mother. No longer suckling, all three were sleeping peacefully.

Maggie spread open the newspaper and folded the edges backward into a kind of plate. Before approaching, she wanted the mother cat to smell the food. As she lowered the shellfish into the box, the silvery gray cat never took her eyes off Maggie.

"Here you go. I don't know exactly what these things are." Maggie picked up a crustacean by the tail and lowered it back down. "They s-sort of look like crawdads. But whatever. I think they look like something you'd like to m-munch on. And I know what you probably want now: p-privacy. I know the feeling. Enjoy!"

Maggie backed away. She backed all the way to the apartment door and listened.

Soon she could hear crunching noises coming from inside the box.

After dinner Maggie cleared the table and went to take a bath while her parents washed and dried the dishes. She drew steaming hot water and relaxed back into the old cast iron tub. When the water was off, she could hear her parents' voices over the sounds of clinking china. One of the best things about living in such a tiny space was the high quality eavesdropping.

"I can't imagine we're going to run into too many obstacles," her mother was saying.

"From what you're telling me, it sounds like everyone's good to go."

"It's true. Ramsey's got his financing in place. The site is logistically perfect. And the government here wants to see this happen. I think my job is basically to keep everything moving along. Henry says things can get dicey for us when the American side is ignorant of local ways, but—"

"Henry?"

"Baumsdorfer. Henry Baumsdorfer is my immediate superior at the embassy. He's good but a little too accommodating for my taste. I wouldn't want to know the kinds of things he tends to sweep under the rug for the sake of globalization, which generally means, 'whatever American interests want.'"

"Hm."

"Then again, if I've learned anything over the years, it's that I can't avoid peeking under that rug eventually. I can shrug it off for a while, it's just that today..."

"Something smells already?"

"Well, not exactly, but—"

"What is it, Elizabeth?"

"It's just that I'm a bit concerned about Ramsey."

"How so?"

Maggie was always interested when her parents spoke freely about other adults, especially when she sensed a criticism coming. She strained to catch every word.

"Let's just say that Ramsey seems utterly ignorant of local ways," Elizabeth said. "As Henry says, things could get awfully unpleasant if Ramsey pushes the wrong buttons. This deal will probably take considerable finessing."

Paul let it go. He knew his wife too well to push. "What's the name of that town where the factory is?"

Elizabeth chuckled before she answered.

"Zagazig. I almost laughed out loud when the Minister said it in my office. I'm still not used to these names."

"I thought you said something like that. Zagazig."

"I'm told the place was named for a particular fish found in that part of the delta."

Silence. Maggie said the name of the town quietly to herself: "Zagazig." And again. "Zagazig." It felt like a magical incantation, like *open sesame* or *abracadabra*.

Elizabeth spoke again.

"Now about you. I'm glad you had a good time today. But I'm concerned: are you going to have enough time and space to get done what you need to get done? We're pretty tightly squeezed in here. How often do you have to check in with the Living World people? What deadlines have they given you?"

"Well, we left it that I'd submit a bunch of samples by the end of November. So I've got plenty of time. I'm making sketches everywhere we go. And I'm thinking Maggie and I will take it one day at a time to the end of this first month and then see where we are. I know she's got to keep up with her class, but maybe it wouldn't be so bad to let her imagination just roam free while we're here. You know, let her read some history and myth on her own."

"But that's not okay, Paul. She can't let everything go. We told the school she'd keep up with her class. If we can't do it ourselves, we'll have to enroll her in the American school here. A couple of people over at the main embassy do that. I know Henry's sons are there."

Maggie groaned. That was definitely the last thing she wanted to do, deal with a whole new batch of 13-year-olds, with all their cliques and quirks. Plus, how would she ever get time alone to explore Cairo if she had to be in school all day? What was the point of traveling halfway around the world just to sit in front of a chalkboard and listen to sarcasm, American-style? *Hey, Maggie, nice bangs. Yeah, right. Like you're some kind of bang expert. Hey Maggie, way to drop that pass. Yeah, right.*

Maggie figured her dad—Mr. Soak Up Local History—would take her side on this one. She listened for her father's objection on her behalf, but it didn't come, at least not yet. Maggie knew that was his way. Paul would listen to her mom's objections, then wait for her to get tied up in work so that she couldn't intervene at the critical moment. Then again, the stakes had never been this high before. What if he couldn't get his work done? What if Maggie's brain went to mush and she couldn't remember the difference between a fraction and a factorial? Hello, Cairo Middle School.

"Maggie!"

"Yeah, Mom?"

"Are you okay in there? It's very quiet."

"I'm f-fine."

It was time to get out of the tub, but she just couldn't. There was so much to think about: the obelisk that had her initials written on it, the flow of people toward mosques under the dazzling noon sun, the cats down the hall. Now she was also worried: how was she going to avoid going to school here? Clearly, she would have to prove that she could work on her own. As soon as she got out of the tub she'd ask to get on-line in order to make an entry in the journal she was keeping for her class and teachers. At least that would be a start.

Maggie lay still as stone. Her hands floated just above her belly; like twin islands, her two big toes broke the surface of the water down by the faucet. It was weird to think that the remnants of the dark purple polish she'd put on in Washington, D.C. were still on her toenails here in Egypt. And she still had the V of tan lines along her feet from wearing flip-flops all summer. Between her toes the cold water dripped slowly. Concentric ripples spread between her feet.

Maggie gave her submerged body a once-over to check if there were any new developments she should be aware of. She stared, hypnotized by the tiny pearls of underwater bubbles that collected around her navel.

Hi, Everybody!

Maggie was now cool and clean. She had towel-dried her hair and brushed out the tangles. Dressed in her favorite tee shirt and cotton paisley lounging pants, she sat with the laptop to compose her journal entry for English class. Where to begin? She took a sip of iced mint tea and turned away from the screen to look out the street-level window. Maggie watched the tops of the heads of people walking by.

I'm sorry it's been a few days since I've written to you guys. One of the reasons I haven't written is that there is so much to describe. It's kind of overwhelming.

So I can tell you something kind of intense. When I come home from a day of touring around—like I did today—I wiped my face off with a Kleenex and the tissue was completely black with soot and grime that had stuck to my skin. I don't tell you this to be gross or anything. It's just that the air here is very polluted. It's polluted because the cars and buses have practically no emissions controls set for them. And the factories don't have controls on what they emit, either. This part is pretty sad, I think. Someone the other day told me that breathing the air here is like smoking a pack of cigarettes a day. Maybe one of you can tell Mrs. Rubenstein in Health this week that it isn't easy for a kid in Cairo to "just say no" to breathing. Just kidding. But you get the picture. The dirt is everywhere.

Maggie paused and looked out the window. This was disturbing stuff. Why was she writing about it?

On the other hand, there's no getting away from the ancientness of this place. You can't really ever forget that people have been living here for thousands, not hundreds, of years. Cars and factories are just the latest thing, and kind of the most superficial thing. This morning I saw an old man walking off to pray, just shuffling along through the sunshine in his scuffed up leather slippers right past a huge pink granite obelisk that's been standing in the same place for...wait, I'll have to do some math here...roughly 3,943 years. And still, even the old things are surrounded by so much life. Cats especially. I've never seen so many cats wandering freely in the streets.

By the way, can someone please download the class picture for me when it comes out? Also, a picture from the apple-picking field trip. That sounded totally fun. I'll send you guys pictures from here in the next few days. Bye for now!

—Maggie

Lying in bed that night, Maggie stared up at the complex pattern of cracks in the white ceiling plaster. She liked to imagine that these seemingly random cracks actually represented a map of an imaginary world. Only she could interpret the borders that defined the states, lakes, rivers, and secret hideaways of the creatures who inhabited the land. In this game, which she played every night after reading, Maggie fantasized about being the first Earthling to visit the land mapped above her head. Who should live there tonight? Dragons? Witches? Unicorns? Cats? Yes, cats. A land ruled by cats, with comfortable ledges worn into the sides of every bluff, and cozy hollowed-out places just right for napping. Small shady lakes were filled with fresh cream, and naturally chilly caves contained plentiful stocks of raw salmon and tuna. As Maggie tried to work out the details, her eyelids grew heavier. In minutes, she was asleep on her back in perfect mummy position.

Chapter 5
The Figurine

MAGGIE HALTED IN HER TRACKS. Just inside one of the Northern Cemetery's low-walled tombs, a person was trying to get her attention. It was an old woman. The woman's lined and leathery face, framed in a navy scarf decorated with large red flowers, seemed to be summoning her. Maggie watched closely. Squatting beside a charcoal brazier, the woman extended her right arm with the palm facing up. Keeping all four fingertips together, she opened and closed her hand several times quickly in a beckoning gesture. A gold bangle slipped from her wrist down into the dark sleeve of her shapeless dress. Maggie instantly recognized her as the woman who sold chickens and pigeons. The one reading the magazine. The one with the calico cat.

"*Salam 'alekum. Ahlan wa sahlan.*"

"Dad, she has a market stall near our apartment. Mom and I saw her yesterday. What's she s-saying?"

"Not sure, Mag."

"She says, please to be our guests and stay yourselves for a cup of tea and a morsel of the fresh *hamam* which now she cooks."

The broken English came from a far corner of the enclosure, where an old man in a pale blue *galabiyya,* an ankle-length cotton shirtdress, sat on a low painted stool. The old man's brown hands held a leather-bound *Qur'an,* which lay open on his lap. Three kids—they must have been the old couple's grandchildren—kicked a soccer ball in a flat sandy area outside the confines of the family's small ochre-colored enclosure. From every direction Maggie heard laughter and shouting. This was the strangest cemetery she'd ever seen.

Having set off that morning into the maze-like complex of tombs that made up Cairo's Northern Cemetery, Maggie and her father had been ambling from tomb to tomb and marveling at the existence of a such a place. In the bright sunshine, the City of the Dead's low golden stone walls resembled lidless shoeboxes arranged on a tabletop. Built to honor the dead of Cairo, this parallel city also housed half a million of the living. Each small section of the cemetery contained both a raised or buried tomb and a living family. People and their meager possessions were crowded into every nook and cranny; residents stuffed their make-shift homes with personal little touches that reflected the individual family's identity. It reminded Maggie of office cubicles she saw at home, only these were homes, not offices, and they were completely outdoors and open to the sky. From downtown Cairo, which shimmered in shades of gray and tan way over to the west, the ever-present car horns sounded like distant geese.

Maggie smiled, searching for words to reply."I think w-we ought to stay," she said, her smile frozen in place.

"I agree. Get ready. I'm going to use a new word." Paul raised his voice.

"*Shukran.*"

Paul bowed his head to the old woman and pressed his palms together at chest height, the closest gesture he could think of to suggest gracious acceptance of her offer. Maggie did the same.

"Well done, Dad."

Maggie picked up phrases more easily than her parents, and was relieved when her father pulled "thank you" out of thin air. Even though she had a feeling the woman was really beckoning to her alone, it wouldn't have been right for Maggie to accept the offer on their joint behalf. Girls just didn't act that way in Egypt.

Maggie stepped over a small ledge that marked the threshold of the tomb. She and her father sat down side by side on the dusty ground and crossed their legs. Maggie looked around. The entire space was about the size of a very large walk-in closet. It had four walls but no ceiling. Along the rear wall stood a cenotaph, a cube-shaped burial stone, which was also used for holding platters, copper pots, and other kitcheny belongings.

"My daughter and I thank you for your invitation." Paul looked at the old woman and then at her husband.

With a black iron fork, the old woman slowly flipped nine or ten pieces of pale tan meat on the grill. Hot juices sizzled into the flame below.

"*Il-hamdu lillah*, thanks be to God, we have enough. With our highly esteemed visitors we share with pleasure," said the old man, who introduced himself as Mahmoud Zuhayri. "My wife you may call Oum."

Maggie turned to the old woman, who was staring at her. Maggie nodded at the introduction. "You from English, yes?" Mr. Zuhayri asked.

"United States of America. My daughter, my wife, and I are living in Cairo for several months. We are very much enjoying your beautiful and fascinating country, Mr. Zuhayri. My name is Paul Underwood, and this is my daughter, Margaret Audrey Underwood."

Maggie noticed the way her father's language turned more formal to match the local custom. He could have been reading lines from a play. Like a stage prop, she sat perfectly still. Normally at home her dad never introduced her to strangers with all three names. Maggie wondered if she'd eventually be able to speak this way, too. Even in three weeks, Maggie had grown used to being a silent companion when men spoke to her father. She listened. She watched. But she didn't say anything. In a way it was nice not having to be spoken to. She never did like facing the annoying and boring questions posed by American adults meeting her for the first time. All they ever wanted to know is what her favorite subject was. What sports she played. Where she thought she wanted to go to college. What she wanted to be when she grew up. As if she knew. It was way easier not having to speak.

While the old man spoke, his wife looked up from her cooking to peer briefly at Maggie. The she turned back to her work. Maggie watched the old woman sprinkle a coppery red powdered spice onto the grilling meat. The food began to smell good.

An ear-piercing shout came from outside the tomb. Maggie stood up and looked over the wall. It was the oldest boy, a serious-faced person about her own age, yelling at his brother for apparently breaking some rule in the game. Maggie watched him scold his younger brother, who took the correction submissively. They resumed the game and Maggie sat back down. There was nothing to do but listen and look around.

Across the enclosure stood a low table covered with a bright blue cloth. The table held an assortment of miniature sculptures and figurines. Maggie could tell that these small items occupied an honored place in the home. The table reminded her of shrines she'd seen in church. Under the table, so still that Maggie almost did not see it, crouched the old woman's calico cat. At first Maggie thought it was sleeping. But all at once the cat stretched open its mouth in a huge, tooth-revealing yawn.

Oum observed the object of Maggie's gaze and put down her grilling fork. She wiped her hands on her black dress and went over to the table. She picked something up and brought it over to Maggie. It was a small bronze figurine cast in the shape of a cat. Maggie took the figurine and held it in her hand. Heavy and solid, it fit easily in her palm. Smooth as polished sea glass, the slim-shouldered cat was sculpted in a simple sitting position—forelegs straight, back haunches folded. Its tail was wrapped snug around the base on its right side. Tiny golden hoops adorned its nose and ears. An elaborate ornamental necklace was carved around its neck; the necklace showed an owl with spread wings. In Maggie's palm, the figurine grew warmer.

"*Da Bastet,*" Oum said in a loud whisper.

Maggie was startled to be addressed. People in Cairo usually didn't talk to her.

"Excuse m-me? *Ana m-mish fahma.* I don't understand."

Oum seemed exasperated. She took the hand in which Maggie was holding the figurine and covered it with both of her own rough yellowish hands. Her long arched nose was inches from Maggie's.

"*Da Bastet. Da—*" She gave Maggie's hand a vigorous pump—"*Bastet.*"

Maggie thought she understood. The woman was trying to tell her that the cat figurine represented something or someone called Bastet. But why didn't she simply ask her husband to translate? Obvious: she couldn't interrupt a man-to-man conversation. Or maybe there was another reason. In any case, Maggie smiled to signal her comprehension.

"Bastet. This is B-bastet. I understand you now."

Oum let go of her hand.

Oddly, Maggie's hand continued to grow warmer. It was as if the bronze were generating some kind of heat on its own. Maggie shifted it into her left hand, but the metal was becoming too hot to hold onto.

"This is w-weird. Ouch."

Oum raised one eyebrow. She observed exactly what was going on, but did not make any offer to take back the figurine. Maggie wanted to show respect, but could hardly hold on another second. Something told her it would be wrong to drop the little cat. Gently, she lowered it into the lap hammock formed by her skirt as she sat cross-legged on the ground. The figurine lay cradled on its side as Maggie looked up into the woman's dark brown eyes.

Oum murmured something in Arabic but Maggie had no idea what the words meant. She hoped she hadn't violated the rules of hospitality. She felt queer, slightly afraid, and cut off from her father under the penetrating gaze of the old woman. What was going on?

About three minutes went by before Oum—who spent the whole time staring at Maggie—removed the figurine from Maggie's skirt and replaced it on the table. Without another word she returned to her grill and squatted down. Taking up her iron fork, she speared the meat onto a tin plate and hollered outside for the boys. She murmured something under her breath and the calico cat stepped out from under the table and left the enclosure.

Mr. Zuhayri poured sweet syrupy tea flavored with mint into seven small glasses. He handed them out to his family and guests. Maggie was grateful for a sip of something.

Oum smiled for the first time as she passed Maggie the platter. Obviously, whatever had happened with that strange hot figurine was not all bad.

"This smells wonderful," Paul said, taking up a piece of meat with the *'eish baladi,* the pita, that his hostess arranged in a circle around the tin platter. "What have you made this morning? I believe I heard you say *hamam*. What is *hamam* in English?"

"*Hamam* is in Egypt one of our delicacies," Mr. Zuhayri said, as his hungry boys devoured their portions. "I believe for this fowl the word in English is pigeon."

Pigeon.

Another one of those strange days, Maggie said to herself, chewing silently. She was eating a piece of cooked pigeon. Flying rodent. Flapping nuisance. And the really weird thing was, it tasted delicious.

"To my wife I was just explaining that this morning we are favored with the presence of an artist," Mr. Zuhayri said, as the group sat eating. Oum nodded. She seemed to be able to understand a bit of English, Maggie noticed, but did not say anything herself.

An airplane passed by overhead, angling up and off to the west with a roar. When the deafening sound of the jets had diminished, their host continued.

"In our most ancient tradition, artists formed the bridge between the sacred and the profane. They connected the world of gods and spirits to the world of this—the world of grilled *hamam* and dust beneath our feet."

"Exactly!" Paul said excitedly. "I do like to think that my work also forms connections. Right now I am working in collage. I take the bits, scraps, and discarded objects of our daily lives and work them into a large canvas. I try to make the pattern appealing to the eye, but also revealing to the soul. I am finding a great deal to work with here in Cairo."

Their host nodded. "Yes, Mr. Underwood, our streets probably are richer in materials than in America yours are. We Egyptians like to let things lie where they fall. Either we build right over them, or someone passes by and picks them up as treasure. America, they say, is new and clean. How do you find the material you need?"

"America only seems clean, Mr. Zuhayri. We make garbage just like everyone else. Unfortunately, I don't have all day to scavenge. I teach school for a living, as most artists have to do in our country. Perhaps our society doesn't treasure the artist as much as we might. And we have bills to pay in the profane world just like anybody else."

Their host nodded. Maggie noticed that Mr. Zuhayri nodded a lot. But it wasn't just a "yes" nod. It was more of a small, repeated bowing of the head. It seemed like a way of saying that he was listening with respect.

Maggie listened, too. Her thoughts were whirling. Treasure and trash. Somehow it had to stay in balance. That's what always bothered her about some of the kids at school. They seemed to forget there was anything else but all the stuff and gadgets you could buy. Clothes, CDs, cell phones, movies, candy, french fries, earrings, video games, computer games, TV shows. But there were also kids who rebelled against the popular crowd by acting like there was nothing meaningful about the material world at all. All that mattered to them was what couldn't be seen. Abstract ideas like Truth, Honor, Love, Nature, Time, Peace. Those types drove her no less crazy. How could you know about Love if you didn't pay attention to the flesh-and-blood details of the person you loved, including the jewelry in their earlobes? Neither type lived in balance. Both were extreme. Was it possible to live in the real world but still have sacred space? Not sacred like a church, but sacred space exactly wherever you happened to be. Sacred space everywhere all the time, sacred space that shared the day-to-day space. Maggie twirled her pony tail with one finger. When she looked up from the ground, she caught the eye of the serious-faced eldest grandson. He looked away quickly.

Oum saw that the children were finished eating and brushed them back out to play.

Mr. Zuhayri set up his *sheesha,* a kind of water pipe, to have a smoke. Oum delivered hot coals from the grill while Mr. Zuhayri placed fresh tobacco in a little clay pot to be inserted in the pipe. Maggie studied the contraption, guessing it was sort of like a bong, although she'd only heard about bongs secondhand in jokes and movies. The glass of the water bowl was shaped like a miniature bowling pin. The lower half was a deep emerald green and the top was clear. A spindly brass stem rose from the glass, and a green and blue hose snaked from the base of the pipe to Mr. Zuhayri's lips. Actually, Maggie thought, the pipe reminded her of a musical instrument. Only instead of blowing into it, Mr. Zuhayri sucked out until it gurgled. Musical smoke.

Maggie's father was explaining the reason for their move to Cairo.

"My wife, Elizabeth Amy McKee, is with the United States government. She is here working on a project that brings together businessmen from Egypt and our country. A cotton factory is looking for foreign investors. Your government wants to expand the facility in order to help it be more productive."

"And where is this factory?"

Paul turned to his daughter. "Mag, help me out. What's the name of the town Mom told us last night? Oh shoot, I think you were in the other room."

"You m-mean Zagazig?

"That's it. It's a place northeast of here called Zagazig."

"Ah, yes," said Mr. Zuhayri. "With Zagazig I am familiar."

Oum said something to her husband in Arabic. He answered simply with one affirmative word.

"Aywa."

To Maggie's shock, Oum gasped and cried out, wringing her hands in evident dismay. At the same time, and for no apparent reason, the small cat figurine fell from the edge of the table to the sandy ground. It landed with a small muffled thump.

Chapter 6

Balancing Acts

"SHEESH, DAD. THAT WAS t-totally intense. Did you see the way she looked at me as we left?"

"I did."

"It was like she wanted me to do something or s-say something. What was that all about, anyway?"

"I have no idea, Maggie. It seemed to get especially bizarre when she heard about the plans for Zagazig."

"Maybe she has family there or something."

"'Or something' is right."

Maggie and her father had left the Zuhayris. Exploring another section of the cemetery, they were walking on Sultan Ahmed toward the mausoleum of Ibn Saleem, which had been their original destination that morning. Now that they were alone, Maggie wasn't sure if she should say anything to her dad about what had happened when she was holding the figurine of Bastet, that little cat. After all, she might have been imagining the heat. Then again, it certainly felt like a real enough burn. Not a flashing, blistering kind of burn you get from an explosion or a splash of boiling water, but a more smoldering heat, the kind that slowly grows hotter and hotter over time, like a fever.

On all sides Cairenes were gathering in noisy groups of picnickers. It was a Friday, the customary moment in the week for daytripping to the tombs and having a festive lunch with the spirits of your dead family members. Braziers smoked, and cats roamed silently up and down the streets looking for bits of cooked chicken and salted fish. Maggie noticed the bright colors of everyone's clothing—so vibrant against the sandy hues of the tombs and the solid black of the Muslim women's gowns. She watched the men jest and slap each other on the back. She observed the hushed and deferential subservience of the women, who raised their voices only to scold or applaud a child's antics.

How different were so-called eternal resting places back home. Maggie pictured the cemetery where her grandparents were buried. A solemn, sterile, manicured expanse of green maintained by backhoes and weed whackers. The only two times she had ever visited the place were for the funerals of Grandpa Morris and some great aunt she never really knew, and those ceremonies were miserable and brief. Along the way to their family plot, clumps of real and fake flowers told of visitors to neighboring plots. Horrible carpets of plastic grass tried to mask the fact that people were actually being lowered into holes dug in brown dirt. By day, a cluster of people in dark suits and dresses might gather around a single plot or two; but at night the cemetery lay isolated and lifeless. Without knowing exactly why, Maggie had always been troubled by cemeteries. Now she began to figure it out. Graveyards and graveyard stories made people imagine only scary things—ghouls, witches, goblins, ghosts. All the creatures that make people scared of death. It was disturbing just thinking about entering a cemetery, about having to pass through a black wrought iron gate or a stone wall to get where the dead people were. No, the American cemetery certainly wasn't the kind of eternal resting place *she* wanted, all cut off from everyone. Here in Cairo, the living and the dead were, well, connected.

Maggie observed the crowds, listened to the tinny music from transistor radios, and smelled the aroma of frying balls of *taamiya,* the chickpea paste people put into their sandwiches. Here the living and the spirits of the dead shared close quarters, side by side. Maybe this was the way things were supposed to be. Maybe this was one way of keeping things in balance, like her Dad was saying to Mr. Zuhayri.

Maggie started taking a closer look at the cats. They were everywhere. Everywhere. Walking around in that mute, dignified way, as if balancing on a tight rope. Eating, grooming themselves, sleeping in the sun, playing in alleys with bits of paper and plastic, curled up behind walls. Maggie thought about the family of cats she'd discovered yesterday by the mailboxes. She thought about the trio of cats in Heliopolis. Even the calico cat at Oum's, which seemed like a typical street cat, but also like a member of the family.

She thought about the Bastet figurine that heated up in her hand and tumbled to the ground for no reason.

"You know, Dad. I think I could write an ess-s-s...report about all the cats of Cairo. A descriptive, English essay type thing to turn in for my term paper in December. I could study the history of cats in Egypt, and describe how they live day to day. Kind of a combined Social Studies and English paper. Do you think my teachers w-would approve?"

Still worried about being sent off to the school for expat American kids, Maggie hoped another formal assignment might finally convince her parents that taking this year off was fine. The thing was, cats genuinely interested her.

"Hm, Mag. I think you may be onto something there. Do you think you could generate enough material for a term paper?"

Encouraged, Maggie spun out a few ideas.

"Even those cats today seem w-worth a story, Dad. I've noticed m-more cats in one day here than in thirteen years in D.C. Also there's that weird thing about my initials on the obelisk. And if I pull images off the Internet, and m-maybe interview people about their cats..."

Paul nodded along. "As long as this is properly done, I guess it's academically legitimate," he said. "We'll have to see how it goes, though."

Maggie felt parched.

"Dad, I could use a drink before we head over to mom's office. Do you have a b-bottle on you?"

Leaning back against a hot grainy stone wall, Maggie guzzled water for a full minute. On the other side of the wall, a cheer rose up from the fans watching a graveyard soccer game. Maggie turned to watch too. She thought about the jillions and jillions of soccer games she'd played at home. Games played on soft mowed grass and refereed by capable adults blowing whistles. Everyone had to play with cleats, with shin guards, with bright-colored uniforms, with mouth guards. Any kid would be booted off the field if she didn't wear even one of these items. Here the game was played barefoot on brown dirt by a ragtag bunch of men and boys of various ages. The under-inflated ball was smudged with grime. Nothing could be more different. And yet the cheers from the sidelines sounded just like the cheers Maggie heard at home.

"I'm ready to get going now," Maggie said, recapping the water bottle. "We can wait around for mom until she's ready to leave for lunch."

Elizabeth was hosting a meeting in a first-floor conference room when Maggie and Paul arrived hot and worn out from the street. Neither one had wanted to face formal introductions after a long morning of touring, so they dodged directly and quietly into a side area used as storage space. A flimsy partition that folded open and shut like a paper fan was all that separated this space from the conference room. Maggie collapsed in an office chair next to the street-level window. Paul immediately tipped back in another one, rested his feet on a stack of file folders, and closed his eyes.

Just as Maggie began to tune into the voices in the adjacent conference room, a shape leaped onto the windowsill from outside. Maggie was so startled it took her a moment to realize that the shape was a cat. Not only that, it was Oum's calico. Maggie relaxed and smiled. The cat meowed quietly and Maggie reached over to pet it. The fur was so soft, she scooped the animal into her lap. The cat knit its claws up and down in the khaki fabric of her skirt before settling down comfortably.

Maggie noticed that if she looked at the window from a particular angle, she could see a perfect reflection of the room on the other side of the partition. Without being seen herself, she had a clear view of the profiles of two men. Dimly, she could even see her mother.

The meeting included William Harrison Ramsey II, the head of SPR & Sons Textiles, and Mr. Farouk Moussa, the director of Delta Cotton Company, Ltd. Delta Cotton owned the mill in Zagazig. The men had asked to come in before the formal meetings next week with Shawqui Mahfouz, the trade minister, and Henry Baumsdorfer, Elizabeth's supervisor in the State Department. There were details to be ironed out before a formal, international trade contract could be signed.

Although both men were pleased with the pending deal, they couldn't have been more different. A businessman on the scent of imminent fortune, Ramsey was a large man with a red face and white hair. In his fine clothes he looked swollen with anticipated success.

"Cotton is in my blood, sir," Ramsey said to his Egyptian associate. "SPR & Sons has been around since colonial times. Why, my own grammy's mammy Maisie, the colored woman who nursed all the Ramseys of that time, worked fields owned by the Greenvale Ramseys."

Mr. Moussa nodded politely. On the other side of the partition, Maggie rolled her eyes.

"Now although generous," Ramsey continued, "the subsidies currently provided to us cotton men by the government of the U.S. of A. don't go quite far enough, in my humble opinion, to sustain the business into the coming decades—especially with all this doggone protesting coming from third world cotton people. It is my intention to connect SPR & Sons to the global network. You people have the laborers. I have the cold hard cash. And the know-how. It makes good solid sense for us to team up."

The American gave Mr. Moussa a light punch on the shoulder with a balled fist. Maggie saw her mother cringe. Was this guy for real? Grammies and mammies?

Farouk Moussa was a small round man packed like a sausage into tight clothing. He presented a small smile.

"We have more than the laborers, Mr. Ramsey," Moussa said. "We produce cotton that is the envy of growers around the world and has been for centuries. Unfortunately, not since your Civil War, when the Union side blockaded exports from the South, has Egyptian cotton held its own in the global market."

"I see you know your history, Moussa," Ramsey said.

"I know *your* history, Mr. Ramsey. Furthermore, a bigger facility at Zagazig will mean more jobs for local workers. More jobs will put money into the local economy and fan development in the whole delta region. Then Egyptian cotton will take a dominant place on the competitive world stage as a coveted luxury item. Thanks to our partnership, Egypt's time will come again."

Moussa's shiny face, arranged into a theatrical expression of hopeful expectation, seemed eager to please the American.

Ramsey raised his styrofoam cup and took another sip of sweet creamy coffee. Moussa had taken one swallow of tea, but apparently couldn't stomach the weak watery liquid that resulted from a single Lipton bag passing briefly through tepid water.

Ramsey sprawled back in his chair and crossed his legs so that one ankle rested just above his knee. He stretched his elbow to the seat back and dangled his hand casually. The short Egyptian industrialist sat bolt upright in his chair, hands face-down on the tops of his thick thighs.

"I think we've got ourselves a mighty nice partnership in the making," Ramsey said, tipping his head to Mr. Moussa. "What we need to work out, of course, is the percentage of profit that will have to stay right here in old Egypt. Not to mention the terms of the expansion to the west of the existing facility. And I'm sure I'll need little Lizzie here's help when it comes to knowing exactly how free my people will be to come in and do their thing—you know what I mean—when it comes to tearing up unstable sites and laying new foundations."

Maggie felt a shot of pain, as if she'd been given a lava injection directly into her thigh. The heat penetrated through her thin cotton skirt as though a live coal were in her pocket. The calico stood up and jumped back to the windowsill. A second later it was gone.

"Ow, Dad. Ow!" she whispered, getting up and running out of the room.

"What is it? What?" Paul said once they'd reached the outer vestibule and were out of earshot.

Maggie couldn't say for sure. It felt like something was burning a hole in her skirt.

"Do you have something I can p-pull this out with? Hurry!"

Her father passed her a blue and white bandana. "Here!"

Maggie wound the cloth around her hand. She shoved her hand into her pocket and pulled out…the Bastet figurine.

"W-w-what?" she exploded. "How did *this* get here? I saw Oum put it back on the table. I saw it tumble off the table right b-before we left."

The heat slowly subsided, allowing Maggie to take a long look at the bronze cat in the palm of her hand.

"What was it doing in my pocket? And why does this thing get s-s-so hot? And why just now?"

Maggie was all in favor of strangeness, but this was a matter of pain. There was a difference between adventure and danger. Or was there? She felt like throwing the figurine out the window. There was something frightening about it.

Paul leaned down and studied the figurine; it was the first he'd seen of it. He'd been deep in conversation with Mr. Zuhayri when Oum showed the figurine to Maggie, and was certainly unaware of its having mysterious properties involving temperature variations.

"I don't understand, Maggie. What do you mean, hot? Was this thing in the fire or something?"

"No, Dad. It just gets hot. Really hot. F-for no reason. All on its own." Maggie paused. "Oum must have slipped it into my pocket as we left. W-why would she do something like that?"

"Let me see it."

Paul touched the bronze cat gingerly with one finger before picking it up. In his own hand it was no hotter than the inside of a human palm on a Cairo Friday at high noon.

"Maggie, this thing isn't hot. Are you sure there wasn't something else in your pocket? Or that maybe you got stung by something?"

"Of course I'm sure. Look."

She turned her pocket inside out.

"There's no hole or burn mark or anything," she said. "But I felt what I felt. And even if it's cool now, that thing was b-burning hot a m-minute ago. W-what's more, why did Oum's cat follow us here?"

Paul looked confused. "Oum's cat?"

"The calico cat from the Northern Cemetery. Where we ate the pigeon. W-w-while you were asleep it came in and sat on my lap."

"Yeah?" Paul said slowly in his tell-me-about-it suspicious voice.

Maggie concentrated on the last few minutes. "W-wait. I'm trying to think. That guy, that Ramsey guy, he w-was just talking about the project Mom's working on with him. I think he was saying something about tearing n-new foundations or something. I mean, digging unstable sites or something like that. Right then the figurine started to get hot."

Paul regarded the object again.

"This is old," he said finally. "I mean, this is the kind of thing that you usually see in a museum, not in some average person's living room. The level of craftsmanship, the detail—my guess is that this figurine was plundered from a tomb or a buried temple generations ago and just happened to land in that family."

Paul frowned. "We have to return it to Oum."

"But, Dad, she gave it to m-me. And—"

"And what?"

Maggie didn't know how to put her thoughts into words. The minute her father told her she'd have to give it back to Oum, she knew that she had the figurine for a reason. Her impulse to fling away the little cat was entirely gone. In fact, it had given way to a completely opposite attitude toward the strange experience. She was no less afraid of the figurine, but she couldn't part with it either.

"Dad, I think it's trying to t-tell me something."

"I'm not going to humor you, Maggie. Even if it's trying to tell you something, this thing has to be returned. It doesn't belong to you."

Maggie swallowed her objection. She also swallowed her next thought, which was that something mysterious was going on with the cats. Could it be a complete and total coincidence that for the last two days she had been having encounters with cats all around Cairo? And that the figurine in her pocket was also a cat? Maybe Oum could help her understand what was going on. Paul scribbled a note to his wife that they'd gone out again and would meet her at home later in the afternoon. "Go ahead and eat without us," he wrote, then left the note with her assistant.

Oum looked around anxiously when the Underwoods returned a half hour later. Her husband was nowhere to be seen.

Paul tried to apologize for imposing again on her time and hospitality. He looked at Maggie, indicating that now was the moment to show the figurine.

Maggie stepped closer to Oum and extended her hand. She watched Oum's face closely.

"Here. I think this w-wound up in my skirt by accident."

Oum was wary. Seeing nobody nearby she went over to Maggie and folded the girl's fingers around the smooth bronze cat. Maggie squeezed the solid metal firmly. Then Oum put her arm around Maggie's shoulders and indicated by hand gesture that she wanted to speak in private. Maggie never even paused.

"It's okay, Dad. I'll be out in a s-second."

Paul left the enclosure.

Maggie hardly knew what was happening. Oum led her by the hand to the small table where Bastet had been displayed. The woman and the girl sat down very close to one another. For a few moments Maggie regarded the other objects on the table—some pebbles, a few brass trinkets, a candle, and four hammered copper bracelets. The silence was broken by Oum's voice speaking, astonishingly, in heavily accented but fluent English.

"I cannot speak freely about these things in presence of others," she said. "My husband does not approve of my private language studies, and I must not appear to be anything but simple Muslim wife. Poor simple Muslim wife."

She chuckled.

"So we have agreement. One that lasts decades. I can read and learn, but only in secret. This is fair to us both since I find way to help his English when we are alone. But he takes coffee now and smokes with the men and you and I have some minutes."

Maggie's eyes opened wide.

"You suppose," Oum said, "that I passed you my beloved Bastet on purpose. Am I right?"

Maggie nodded.

"Do you have any idea why I did this thing? Answer honestly, my daughter. Do you?"

Maggie nodded again.

"Tell me. Tell Oum why she gave you Bastet."

"Does it have something to do with w-why it got hot in my hand?"

"Good girl. You are honest with me."

"I—" Maggie was afraid of speaking her mind, afraid of sounding foolish, but she felt herself caving in to curiosity.

"I feel like the figure is trying to t-tell me something. Trying to make me do something or say something. I feel like it must have started to burn me for a reason. Just now, when I was at my mom's office, it got even hotter than it did when I was here this morning."

Oum smiled.

"Our Bastet only speaks when the time is right, and when person is ready to hear. You may have been listening for long time, my daughter, but you were not ready to hear. Listening is not always hearing, is it?"

Maggie thought a moment.

"No. And I'm s-sorry for not knowing this, but who is B-bastet?"

"Ah, who is Bastet?" Oum clapped her hands together three times. "Who is our mother? Who is our protector? Who brings joy into the world? Who guards our lives and keeps them in balance from one day to the next, from one month to the next, from one season to the next? Who guides our ways of pleasantness from the high ground of her temple in Tell Basta? Ah, who but Bastet?"

Oum was practically chanting these words. It was like listening to a song, or a prayer. Oum's face looked up to the banner of blue sky above their heads and smiled. It was a smile of joy, as if she were remembering something sweet. But what was she remembering? Maggie needed to hear more.

"So Bastet was a g-goddess?"

Oum looked down from the sky at the pale foreign face beside her. She looked into Maggie's wide, green eyes, gazed at the darkening band of freckles spreading like wings across the girl's nose and along the upper curve of her cheeks. Her hair was so smooth and straight, her arms so slender and relaxed in her lap.

"Yes, Bastet was goddess," she finally said. "A goddess from the ancient days, from the days many thousands of years before Islam came to Egypt. She has the head of a cat and the body of a woman. Her guiding force and principle is something very complicated, but also something very simple. I suppose in English you would call it Love. But it is also more than Love. It is Nature herself. We call this the *ba* and the *ka* of the universe."

Maggie opened her hand and brought out the figurine. She gave it a long look.

"But you said this was Bastet. To me it looks like a cat, a regular cat. It doesn't have the b-body of a woman at all."

"Ah," said Oum. "I think you are being too—what is your word in English for this?—too literal. Bastet's agents are the cats, but her agents are also the people living in harmony with her spirit."

Maggie had about a million questions, and all of them fluttered at her lips. She shuffled through the various unknowns in order to put them in some kind of order. At least two seemed most pressing right now. Why did Oum cry out when she heard that Maggie's mom was working on a project at Zagazig? And way more nerve-wracking, why was Bastet communicating with an ordinary American girl? Unfortunately, just as the first question took shape,

Oum seemed to shrink back into her inexpressive pose. Sure enough, Maggie saw Mr. Zuhayri enter the tomb.

"For you your father waits," he said brusquely. "He draws on his paper many pictures, but now he is ready to walk on."

Oum hastened head-down to the other side of the tomb to prepare her husband's *sheesha.* Filling his water pipe marked the beginning of her afternoon. For the second time that day Maggie took her leave. This time she knew what she had in her pocket, even if she didn't have the vaguest idea why it was there.

Chapter 7

Prompts

EARLY THAT EVENING IN THE dusky apartment hallway, Maggie sat cross-legged with her back against the cool plaster wall. The Bastet figurine lay in her lap. Maggie peered down into the brown Nike box where the gray striped cat was grooming her kittens. Up and down the mother cat's head bobbed. From one direction to another her tongue rubbed against the nap of fur along the flanks, legs, necks, heads, and paws of the infant cats. For a moment the cat looked up at the ceiling as if startled. Maggie looked up too but saw nothing except peeling paint. The gray cat returned to her work.

Maggie knew she ought to be heading out to buy three bottles of mineral water and a bag of fresh pita. Only today, after nearly a month of regular pleading, had Maggie been granted permission to go out alone on the street and conduct small transactions and limited neighborhood explorations. Maggie knew perseverance was only partly responsible for the victory; her mother's end-of-the-day fatigue made her too weak to object.

"You know I'll be f-fine," Maggie had said.

"I know you'll be fine. Just don't dilly-dally."

But as soon as she walked out the door, Maggie had turned left instead of right. She just had to see what the hall cats were up to, and whether they'd eaten the shellfish she'd left the night before. Two minutes couldn't make any difference.

There was no sign of the newspaper platter or the grayish pink crustaceans. No sign of any food at all, only three kittens having an evening cleaning. The mother cat opened her mouth.

"M-m-raugh. Mraugh. M-m-meow-ow-ow."

With each sound, Maggie could see the sharp white spikes of the cat's teeth. Although she'd watched Sarah yawn dozens of times, a shiver ran down her spine at the sight of the feral cat's display. Those teeth were needle-sharp. What if this cat had rabies or some other disease? She should know better than to get close to a stray animal in a big city. What was the matter with her? She ought to be keeping her distance from these cats. Cute as the kittens were, their mother might prove to be vicious. Maggie held up the figurine. Could there really be any connection between an old piece of metal and the stray animals by her side?

"M-mraaugh." Louder now.

Why was the gray cat meowing? Could she be speaking to Maggie? Now the hallway seemed very quiet.

Maggie, you are being totally ridiculous. What you have in your hand is a sculpture made a long time ago by some Old Egypt artist. Why it got hot is anybody's guess. Maybe Oum did some kind of magic trick to heat it up. The main thing is that you—Maggie slipped Bastet in her pocket and looked directly at the gray cat—*are an ordinary cat in an ordinary apartment building. You don't know anything about Bastet. It's just a simple coincidence that you came here to our building to stay off the street. All you need to worry about is eating and feeding your kittens. Same with all those other cats. And all I need to worry about is not getting scratched or bitten by a stray cat.*

The cat flicked its tail.

Just to prove to herself that she wasn't afraid, Maggie closed her eyes for a moment. If she were really afraid she'd be too scared to close her eyes.

"*MAU!*"

"What?"

Maggie opened her eyes. Had she really been called by name? Out loud? Or was this all a result of being so far from home, so cut off from the laughter of her friends and the bang of her locker between classes? Now she was really frightened. The best thing to do would be to act completely natural. Maggie got up, smoothed out her skirt, and spoke to the gray cat as she spoke to her own Sarah.

"Look, I'm not sure w-what I can find for you tonight, but I'll come back with something. If worse comes to worse, I'll bring out a little m-milk later."

The gray cat looked away and lowered her eyelids halfway. Her face was more placid than Sarah's, more sober. Sarah was always looking for action. This cat seemed to be storing up energy. The kittens snuggled down and closed their eyes.

Outside it was a mob scene. With just a few minutes to go before sunset prayers, the street vendors were shouting out their wares. Women in head scarves hurried along clutching bags bulging with food. Along the narrow sidewalk men argued and chattered in clumps. From open first- and second-story windows old women shouted orders and reminders to girls and boys doing the evening errands. Maggie turned a corner to get to the small shop where she and her family bought some of their groceries.

Low in the sky, a sliver of moon began to rise. It was a warm evening, and supper time cooking smells were beginning to drift along the street. Maggie was growing hungry and walked a little bit faster. Just as she approached the last street she had to cross, a bus crammed with passengers—some of whom were hanging off the back end—nearly collided with a small red car. The two drivers slammed on their breaks and leaned on their horns. The screech of the wheels and the horn blasts made Maggie's heart jump. Looking up at the scene of the near-accident, she missed her step and tripped over a slimy piece of cantaloupe. She fell down like a chopped tree.

In a moment Maggie was surrounded by pedestrians jabbering at her in Arabic. She had no idea what anyone was saying, but she was pretty sure that they were trying to make sure she was okay. Apart from two scraped palms and a skinned right knee, she appeared to be fine. The two drivers were now yelling at one another, and the passengers of the bus were yelling at their driver to forget about it and keep on going.

"I'm okay," Maggie said, looking around and smiling. "R-really."

She held up her hands in proof, but people continued to gather. The attention was worse than the fall. She didn't want to seem rude, but she wanted to break free of well-wishers and rubberneckers. After about a minute, a boy about her own size pushed through the crowd. He was wearing a stained yellow tee shirt and black gym shorts. He was barefoot. Maggie recognized him at once as the eldest of Oum's grandsons. He had bright dark eyes and ragged black hair.

"Hi," Maggie said.

The boy lifted his hand shyly. Maggie marched over to him as if they were long lost friends.

"Do you s-speak any English at all? If you do, please tell everyone that I am p-perfectly fine and would like to m-move along away from here."

The boy smiled. His teeth were white and even. Like a magician waving a wand to make a rabbit disappear, he spoke aloud and the crowd dispersed. Maggie was so pleased she actually clapped her raw palms together.

"Ouch! That was great. Thanks! My name is M-maggie."

"I am Tareq."

Maggie and Tareq continued in the direction Maggie had been heading when she tripped.

"I was just going to buy a few things."

"I see. I come with you?"

"Sure."

Tareq, Maggie learned, had been at work collecting trash—plastic bags, aluminum cans, bottles, rags, and cardboard boxes, all the stuff that collected on the street during a typical day. Later on he would sell as much of it as he could to the garbage dealers. In Cairo there was a buyer for everything. Many children worked as professional scavengers, turning a profit from the flotsam and jetsam that floated across their paths. Their families depended on this income.

At the grocer's Maggie found the water and took a plastic bag of pita from a large basket on the counter. She opened her change purse and withdrew enough *piastres* to cover the purchase. Seeing the full load of Egyptian currency, Tareq watched her wide-eyed. Maggie noticed.

"Is there anything you need, Tareq? I feel like I owe you a reward for getting me out of that s-situation. For all I knew they were about to throw me in an ambulance and take me to the hospital."

Tareq laughed.

"No, those people were not ever thinking to do that. They say that your shoes are not good for walking streets. Straps weak on sandals. Women also said you are too skinny, ankles like river reeds."

Now it was Maggie's turn to laugh.

"And I thought they were concerned for my w-welfare!"

"Welfare? You mean for the government to take care of you when you do not work?"

"Wow. Impressive vocab there. No, I just mean that I thought they were worried about my fall and whether I hurt m-myself. But never mind. How do you know about w-welfare, Tareq?"

For some reason Maggie wasn't self-conscious about her stammer around Tareq. He didn't even seem to notice it.

"Oh, we have the friends who have the satellite dish. Not their own, but the connections are made in secret with wires. My grandmother will let me watch the CNN sometimes. She wants me to speak the right English for when I can get a good job in Gezira Sheraton."

"That sounds like a good idea," Maggie said. "But I think you already speak very good English, Tareq." She looked at the array of sweets before her. Honeyed nuts. Halvah. Hard candies wrapped in cellphane. "W-would you like something while we're here? Gum? Chocolate?"

Tareq turned serious.

"I would like nothing here."

By his tone Maggie couldn't tell if her new acquaintance meant "here," as in "here in the shop" or "here" as in "here in Cairo." He repeated himself.

"I would like nothing that is here. I would like instead to have talks with you. Maybe you will spend the time talking to me and I will show you some places in Cairo you have not seen."

They left the shop and started back toward Maggie's apartment. As they walked Maggie looked down and compared her own sandaled feet to the bare, calloused feet of this boy who lived in a roofless tomb and collected garbage for a living. She could hardly believe what was happening.

Meanwhile, her palms and knee were beginning to sting. Maggie knew she ought to get back in a hurry to wash out the dirt. But Tareq's proposal was more than intriguing. A kid her own age willing to show her around. She wouldn't have to be squired about by her father all the time like some sort of pet. After all, her dad had his own art to think about, his own Cairo to explore. Maggie had been wanting to find a way of living here for herself. Maybe this was a first step. If nothing else, she'd see things other Americans never get to see. She turned and gave Tareq's hand a strong shake.

"I think we've got ourselves a deal," she said. "My f-fascinating conversation in exchange for your guidance."

"I find you again soon," Tareq said.

After dinner Maggie checked her e-mail to see the week's writing prompt from home. She eyed her inbox until she saw her English teacher's name, then clicked open the message:

Describe an object in your life that you treasure. What is it? Describe it in great detail. How did you acquire it? Why is it special to you?

Maggie thought about the subject and had to laugh. Here she was in an apartment ten thousand miles away from her bedroom and any treasure she might have there. She had never had a special blanket or baby doll. She did have Sarah, though. She could probably write a whole book about Sarah. But a pet didn't seem to capture what her teacher meant by treasure. She looked away from the screen and glanced around her temporary home. The star-shaped earrings James gave her at the end of sixth grade lay in an ashtray by the sofa. They were pretty special to her. A gift from her first boyfriend and all. Maggie shook her head. She had just spent a chunk of time with a boy who barely had clothes on his back. She couldn't help but wonder what Tareq would write in answer to an American English teacher's writing prompt. Then it dawned on her how she needed to reply.

A treasure came into my life just this afternoon. It's a cat figurine made of bronze and it was given to me by an old woman who makes her home in an open tomb. You read that right. She lives in a tomb. She has three grandsons and a husband.

Maggie went on to describe the detailed carvings on the Bastet figurine before getting to the heart of the assignment.

I treasure this small object for several reasons. First, it came to me in a strange way. This woman snuck it into my pocket without telling me. Second, it is the symbol for a goddess that many people here still believe in even though it's been a long time since people actually worshipped her in public. And third....

Maggie changed her mind. She had intended to write about the figurine getting hot. Oum had encouraged her to believe that the figurine had somehow chosen her, Maggie. Even Maggie suspected this to be true. But something stopped her from sharing this part. It seemed too private. Too bizarre. As she collected her thoughts, Maggie heard a faint meow from out in the hall. The kittens! She had completely forgotten to bring something back for the cat family. She'd rushed in the door, washed out her cuts, and sat down to dinner. The poor cats had never even crossed her mind. Maggie saved her e-mail as a draft and went into the kitchen.

"Are you still hungry?" Elizabeth asked.

"No."

Maggie realized that she had no excuse to leave the apartment with a dish of milk or a scrap of the cooked chicken they'd had for dinner. She couldn't even really explain to her mother why she was in the kitchen. That "no" was just hanging in mid-air. Should she wait until after her parents went to bed to take the food and water out? Should she tell her mom about them and risk being told to leave feral cats alone? Sneaking out in the night seemed rather drastic. Then again, she didn't want to be forbidden to care for the cats, particularly in light of...she didn't even know what to call it, exactly... in light of the peculiar events of the day. Maggie looked at her mom; Elizabeth was still hunched over papers and memos. Standing by the sink Maggie pulled Bastet out of her pocket. She looked at the figurine, then tucked it away again.

Maggie went to the bathroom and fished out of the hamper the peach-colored tee shirt she'd worn the day before.

She went to the kitchen and took the milk out of the fridge. She poured a few tablespoonfuls into a small saucer. She tore a small handful of chicken meat off a leftover thigh and shredded that into the milk. She filled a second saucer with tap water. Maggie worked quietly, put everything away, and then slipped to the front door carrying the two saucers and the dirty tee shirt.

"I'll be right back, Mom," she called, hurrying past the living room. "I think I dropped s-something on my way in tonight. Back in a second."

Maggie approached the rear of the hall. The kittens were lying on the bottom of the box as usual, but the mother was not. Wide awake and watching with moon-round eyes, the kittens rose to sniff at the meal. One of them scratched at the cardboard with tiny claws.

"M-mau, mraugh."

"You're welcome. I hope you're not too hungry. Is your mom out hunting for you because she thought I'd forget to come? Maybe this can t-tide you over 'til she gets back."

After setting down the food, Maggie reached down into the carton and spread the tee shirt into the small square where the mother cat usually lay to suckle her family. To get it to line the bottom of the carton, she had to gently rearrange the kittens. Maggie could tell the shirt had been worn on a hot Cairo day. It reeked.

"This should m-make me more familiar to you," she said, smiling at the soft kittens, every one of which she was dying to hold. "Let's make sure your m-mom knows she can trust me. I wish I could stay and keep you company, but if I don't go back my own mother will come after me. I'll see you guys t-tomorrow."

Maggie was back in the apartment with the door shut behind her before she realized that things had changed between herself and the cats. First, she was no longer afraid of them; and second, she was sure that her possession of the Bastet figurine had something to do with their care.

Chapter 8

Various Messages

MAGGIE WAS SURPRISED TO HEAR the next morning that her mom planned to go to work. It was a Saturday.

"What for?"

"It's that Bill Ramsey. He had his people back home fax us some important papers late yesterday, legal documents. I have to be familiar with them before our meetings next week. I wish I didn't have to but I do."

Maggie moaned. Then she had an idea.

"Can I come w-with you? I could hang out and check e-mail. Your computer there is so much faster and I forgot to send my journal response yesterday. It's still saved as a draft."

"Sure. Be ready to go in a half hour. While we're over there, maybe we can do something fun afterward. Paul?"

Paul peeped over the top of his *Egyptian Mail,* the Saturday edition of the daily English-language newspaper. He rattled the large, black-and-white broadsheet. "I think after this I'd like to head out alone."

An hour later Maggie and Elizabeth left the apartment. When Elizabeth went back inside to get her sunglasses, Maggie couldn't help but trot down to the mailboxes to see if she could catch a glimpse of the cat family. The kittens were all there in the carton, snugly humped in the folds of Maggie's tee shirt. The mother cat was still gone. Seeing her shirt there, Maggie felt that a piece of herself was helping to nurture the kittens in their mother's absence. She turned and walked away, glad that the carton looked like trash and would probably be left alone.

A gentle breeze blew bits of plastic wrappers and leaves along the sidewalk on the way to the Metro station. The sun was rising hot and yellow as usual, and the streets were already filled with Cairenes. At the market *souk* near the Metro stop, early-rising tourists were already hunched over loaded tables trying to decide what to bring home for themselves and their friends. Crammed shops opened directly onto the narrow streets. Spread out on tables and carpets were red and gold slippers; perfumes in cut-glass bottles; polished copperware gleaming in the sun; cotton shifts of blue, red, green, black and plain white with golden stitches down the front; amulets and trinkets depicting images from pharoah times. Maggie heard an American woman trying to barter with a vendor. She caught only a word or two from the negotiation.

"But this isn't even real silver," the woman said.

"*La', la', la',*" the vendor said by way of contradiction, holding a shiny medallion in the palm of his hand.

It was almost ten thirty when Maggie and Elizabeth emerged from underground. A big black tom cat heading in the opposite direction regarded them and continued on its way toward the river. Elizabeth's office was around the corner.

"Mom, w-what's that smell?"

"I don't smell anything."

Maggie made a face as they approached the corner newsstand. "Ugh. It's horrible. And it's getting w-worse. Can you s-smell it now?"

"No. Hang on. I'm just going to pick up a *Newsweek*. Wait for me."

Maggie couldn't wait. The odor drew her along the narrow sidewalk. The smell was disgusting, but she had to find out what it was.

Maggie arrived at the street entrance of Elizabeth's office. She looked down and stared in disbelief. Her hand flew up to cover her nose and mouth.

A knee-high pile of dead fish blocked the doorway. Some of the fish were as big as a ruler, others the size of her hand, a few no bigger than her pinky. Some were freshly killed, some beginning to rot. About half were heads only, with long white and bloody spinal cords curving into finned tails. Loose scales and fish bones were scattered in the pile, as well as dark purplish organs still shiny with life. On many of the fish, the flesh had been torn away savagely. From the look of the gashing wounds, this was not the work of a fillet knife. Glassy, unblinking fish eyes stared up at the sky and down into the ground. Dead fish mouths were rounded into silent O's. A vile sight to match an odious smell.

Maggie stood frozen. Before she could speak, something happened that made her insides heave.

One of the fish, a meaty one with a bloody eye socket, flopped spasmodically in the middle of the pile. In its death throes, one of its gills flapped open and shut three times before finally shutting for good. The fish was dead.

Maggie let out a sound that was part moan, part cry. Elizabeth heard and ran over.

"What is it? What—Oh, my gosh!"

Clamping her hand over her nose and mouth, Elizabeth stared at the pile. A trio of car horns sounded and a police siren screamed by a few blocks away.

"But this makes no sense," Elizabeth finally said. "This isn't a market street. We're the only tenants in this building. Why would a fish monger leave all his unsold stuff here on our doorstep?"

"Mom, look at these things. These are not m-market fish. These are...these are...well, I don't know exactly what to call them. But they are not fit for eating. They're all... d-devoured."

Elizabeth shifted her *Newsweek* into the same hand as her briefcase. She put her arm around Maggie. Maggie continued to stare at the pile of bloody bones and silvery gray corpses.

"We need to find a policeman or somebody," Elizabeth said. "We need to clean this mess up. But you don't, Maggie. Why don't you step over it and go on upstairs. I'll take care of it. Here's the key."

Maggie took the key and mindlessly slipped it into her backpack. While Elizabeth went off to the corner to look for someone in a uniform, Maggie's thoughts were whirling. A small boy Maggie had never seen before came over and crouched down to examine the curling entrails of a river perch. Suddenly, Maggie heard a soft chorus of voices sounding the syllable that was becoming familiar to her now, the syllable made up of her very own initials.

"MAU!"

This time it made the hair on the back of her neck stand on end.

"MAU!"

"What? Where are you?"

Maggie's throat choked up. She could feel her heart beating.

"MAU!"

Maggie looked around. In the shadows of a doorway across the street she saw them: seven cats sitting calmly on their haunches in a close bunch,. One of them, a honey-colored tabby with amber eyes, was licking something gooey off a lifted paw. It drew the paw up to its face, tucked its head down, and began combing fur from ear to mouth. Next to this one was the silvery striped mother cat from Maggie's front hall. No wonder she hadn't been around for Maggie's last two visits. The cat met her gaze.

Nearly frantic, Maggie opened her backpack and dug around for the figurine. Got it! Lifting it out in her hand, Maggie felt the smooth bronze warming to her touch. She raised her eyes from Bastet to the street cats. They watched her calmly. Then one by one, they lay down and rested their heads on their front legs. Watching their display of submission, Maggie trembled.

For what seemed like hours, Maggie stared at the cats across the narrow street. Seven heads lay upon seven pairs of outstretched forelegs. Tails and whiskers were still. Only their ears twitched, now shifting forward, now laying back. Were they waiting for her to do something? Say something? The figurine continued to feel warm in her hand—very warm, but not burning hot. She rubbed her thumb along the back of the talisman. The smell from the pile of dead fish was growing stronger as the sun rose higher in the sky and late morning heat began to rise off the pavement, but Maggie felt less overwhelmed by it somehow. She felt neither disgust nor fear. She knew, deep down in her soul, as if a bright light were shining on a private place where reason and logic held no power, that these cats had been responsible for the fish slaughter. The cats had dumped the fish in front of her mother's office for a reason. As Maggie stood looking at them, she was sure that this reason had something to do with the figurine, with Bastet, and with herself.

Elizabeth's return with an armed policeman broke her concentration.

"He doesn't speak much English," her mom said quietly. "But he's all I could find. I showed him my government I.D. badge and he came pronto."

Maggie looked at the officer. Hanging from a brown leather strap slung across his chest was an automatic assault rifle. A bandolier of ammunition crisscrossed his body in the other direction. He had a small, well-trimmed moustache and a friendly face.

"You see?" Elizabeth said to the officer, sweeping her arm as if to display the pile of fish to the growing number of onlookers. "This is my office. They need to be cleared away. The street needs to be hosed down. Do you understand?"

The officer shrugged. He touched both his hands to his chest and shook his head, as if to say that he was not in a position to take care of this problem. Then he made his right hand into a telephone.

"He's s-saying he can call for help."

But the officer shook his head. He extended an open hand to Elizabeth.

"Check that, Mom, he's saying that *y-you* can call for help."

A small mob of passersby were loudly debating how the fish got to the U.S. embassy annex. One angry man in a dark shift and a long gray-black beard, by appearances a devout Muslim cleric, shouted across the crowd to Elizabeth.

"U.S. go home! U.S. go home! *Kifayah!* Enough!"

"Well, this is ridiculous," Elizabeth said. "Come on, Maggie, let's go on up and make the calls we need to make. Give me back the key, please."

The officer used the side of his weapon and sharp words to disperse the crowd. Maggie looked back across the street to the cats, but they had disappeared.

"Now how do you think we ought to get over this mess?" Elizabeth asked. Maggie was considering the problem when she heard her name.

"Maggie!"

"Tareq! Hi! Mom, this is Tareq. Tareq, this is my m-mother, Elizabeth McKee."

Tareq was wearing the same dirty yellow tee shirt and shorts from the day before. He was barefoot again, too.

"I am pleased to make your acquaintance, Mrs. McKee."

Elizabeth shook his hand.

"Mom, Tareq is a friend of mine. I met him with Dad yesterday. We had a s-snack at his house with his family. Remember? I told you about it last night at dinner. Remember?"

Maggie waited for an answer. Tareq broke the silence.

"I will clean for you. Okay?"

"That would be great, Tareq," Maggie said. Even though she was relieved, Maggie was also slightly worried. She was glad to have a local connection to help them with the immediate problem of cleaning up the fish and straightening out the confusion with the policeman, but she definitely did not want Tareq to feel like their personal servant. She didn't want to treat him like hired help. Then Maggie had a thought. What if Oum had assigned Tareq the task of staying close by? What did he know that she did not? Or what did Oum want him to find out about her? There was no way he would have appeared if he hadn't been following her. She was also sure that she needed to ask the old woman a few questions relating to Bastet and the cats. It couldn't be more obvious: the cats were telling her something. But what? Maggie went through the bare facts again in her head. At least seven cats of Cairo had destroyed dozens of fish and deposited them on her mother's doorstep.

"Mom, can I s-stay with Tareq?"

"What?"

"To help clean up. And, I don't know. To just hang out. It's okay. I know how to get around Cairo now. And I know his f-family. Please?"

Tareq nodded.

Elizabeth looked at Maggie and appeared to weigh her options. Maggie's green eyes were alive with sparkling energy.

"Mag, I have a lot of work to do and I don't want to be worrying about you."

"Mom, please! I won't be wandering around the city by myself, and I won't be bothering you while you work!"

After a pause, Elizabeth agreed.

"All right, but let's have a meet-up time and place."

"Let's say home. Home b-by five."

Elizabeth checked her watch. "Sounds good. Listen," she added, moving closer to Maggie and dropping her voice to a murmur. "Have you got your passport?"

"Check."

"A key to the apartment?"

"Check."

"Well, all right, I guess."

"You didn't ask me if I have any money," Maggie teased.

"Do you have any money, Maggie?"

"I've got about a hundred Egyptian pounds and two hundred *p-piastres*. That's...about fifteen b-bucks and change. I can buy lunch. And I can get in a taxi from anywhere. And I won't take the Metro. And I'll look seventeen ways before crossing the street. And I will refuse all unwrapped candy from strangers."

"I guess that just about covers it. Just give me back my key, please."

"Oh, and Mom, can you please p-print out and bring home my e-mail from school and send that draft thing to Mr. Vance?"

"Sure."

Elizabeth turned to Tareq, who was observing the American mother and daughter as if every commonplace expression revealed profound truths of modernity. "So you two will make sure this horrible stuff is gone by the time I come down?"

"I do," Tareq replied. Maggie smiled inwardly at the wrong word. She figured he must have been echoing a vow he once heard on TV.

"Then I would like to pay you for your trouble." She reached for her handbag. Tareq realized what she was doing and backed away.

"No, please, no."

Maggie hoped her mother would not argue and force Tareq to accept the money; he didn't have the language to explain why he didn't want to be paid for doing them a favor. But Elizabeth seemed to know better than to insult the boy's dignity. It was right of her to offer, and right of him to decline.

"Okay, then. Well, I do thank you very much, Tareq." She unlocked the door and went inside, leaving the street door open.

Maggie couldn't believe her luck. She was free! As she turned to Tareq, she realized that she'd been clutching the figurine so tightly her hand was stiff. She put the bronze figurine in her backpack and looked at Tareq.

"Well," she said, nodding toward the smelly heap before her. "W-what now?"

"Now we find bags."

Maggie looked around. "There's an old garbage b-bag over there blowing against the corner of the building."

Tareq ran over to snatch the black plastic bag before it blew down the street. He gave it to Maggie and she held it open. Tareq began scooping fish with his bare hands. He put them in the bag. Maggie had to turn her face away from the smell. Tareq dug through the mass of slime, bones, tails, scales, and fins.

"We need another container," Maggie said, looking around. "Hang on. I'll be right b-back." She put down the full bag and leaped over the diminishing pile into the building. In a few minutes she returned, carrying three more garbage bags and a few paper-covered wire twisties. She tore one of the bags in half. Then she wound the plastic around her hand and knotted it at the wrist so that she had a mitt for handling the dead fish.

"There. I just can't touch this stuff with my b-bare hands."

Tareq shrugged. They worked together until the entire pile was gone. All that remained on the sidewalk was a large watery patch of clear fish scales and a bit of gore.

"N-now what?"

"We put them over there in alley."

"Okay. I'll follow you."

Maggie and Tareq dropped the bags in a heap beside a couple of overflowing garbage dumpsters. Tareq wiped his smeary hands on his shorts.

"Now we walk."

Maggie was thrilled. Finally she was going to be heading around Cairo without her parents. This was exactly what she'd been hoping for all month.

"First we go to river," Tareq said. "I show you river. There we wash hands."

"Whatever you s-say."

Tareq and Maggie set off toward the Nile. As the bell atop the Coptic Christian church began to sound, the Muslim noon call to prayer echoed around the neighborhood. Men crowded into storefronts and unfurled threadbare prayer mats onto the floor. Some of the make-shift places of prayer were too crowded to accommodate the worshippers, and the men spilled out into the street. Stepping off the curb in order to get around the crowds, Tareq and Maggie moved carefully between the legs of prostrated people.

Along the way Maggie got a close-up view of the pinkish brown prune-sized welts in the middle of the men's foreheads; this was the unmistakable sign that they put their heads to the ground five times a day, every single day. Maggie knew the bruises were a sign of devotion. Still, she found the whole idea of religion branding you with a permanent bruise a little disturbing. As she tromped behind Tareq's quick-moving feet, her thoughts drifted to the religious people she knew at home. No matter what the religion was, all of them had to follow so many rules and regulations: eat this, don't eat that; do this, don't do that; say this, don't say that; wear this, don't wear that. Did all these rules move people closer to a sacred place or further away from it? Did rules bring people together or separate them even more? Neither of her own parents was particularly religious, but that didn't mean that Maggie wasn't curious about rituals and beliefs. Maybe one day she could ask Tareq about some of the things she didn't quite understand about Islam.

Finally, in the blazing heat of the day, Maggie and Tareq arrived at the waterfront. As they came out from the shadows of the buildings into the full light falling upon the flowing blue water of the Nile, Maggie noticed that the breeze was stronger here. A steady gust from the north blew her ponytail like a windsock over her left shoulder. Across the broad street called the Corniche el-Nil the river was a deep blue. The water was moving northward, into the wind. The colorful masts of docked feluccas bobbed in the waves.

Arriving on the splintered wooden planks of the dock, Tareq and Maggie both leaned over and scrubbed their hands in the cool water. Tiny bells on the boats clanged and flags flapped against rope. The current gently nudged the colorful, low-lying boats so that they thumped against their moorings.

A nearby felucca bumped the dock. Someone below deck let out a bellowing laugh. He climbed into the sunlight.

"Ahlan wa sahlan!" said a tall man with a huge smile on his dark brown face. His outfit matched the colors of the boat: a red shirt dress over loose green trousers. A red and

silver pillbox hat sat at a jaunty angle on his close-cropped head. Tareq's face, now shiny with perspiration from the long walk, broke into a grin too.

"Nazaret!" he exclaimed. "*Salam 'alekum!*"

"*Wa 'alekum es salam,*" the tall man replied. He opened his arms in a gesture of welcome.

Maggie recognized the man she had met at her mom's office. The driver of that official guy.

"This is friend," Tareq said. "Nazaret, this is Maggie. Nazaret says welcome and hello."

Maggie smiled. "Hi. I think Nazaret and I have m-met."

"We certainly have," Nazaret said. "As I recall, you are the daughter of a most distinguished diplomat. But it is not often that one finds daughters of diplomats on the bank of the Nile."

Maggie knew Nazaret was being friendly, but she still felt embarrassed.

Tareq and Nazaret chatted for a moment in Arabic, and it seemed to Maggie that Tareq was narrating the fish story. Maggie thought she heard the word "embassy." Nazaret's face went serious as he listened. The tall, straight-backed man seemed lost in his own thoughts. Tareq turned back to Maggie to explain.

"Nazaret during week and weekend nights is driver for big Egyptian official. Afternoons and Saturdays he drives felucca for tourist. Boat in family long time. Nazaret Nubian family. Nubians very good on river. Father sick and can no longer sail. So Nazaret pilot."

Maggie nodded. As she tried to make sense of Tareq's explanation, she had a funny feeling that Nazaret was watching her with particular attention.

The docks were packed with people strolling by and snapping pictures of one of the most famous waterways in the world. A middle-aged couple—turned out in tourists' broad-brimmed hats, sturdy walking shoes, and fanny packs tightly cinched around thickened waists—were trying to decide which driver to approach. Normally Nazaret would be calling out for their business, but he was considering the girl before him. Her pale green eyes gazed right back at him. The tourists boarded a neighboring felucca and loudly, with the aid of a phrase book, began negotiating the fee for a ride.

Tareq and Nazaret were talking again. Maggie shifted her weight from one foot to the other and tried to wait patiently for some sign of what they were going to do. She couldn't help but tune in to the conversation of a British mother and daughter stopping behind her. Like recognizing a favorite but long-misplaced sweatshirt in the lost-and-found bin at school, hearing her own language felt serendipitous, a special gift of fate.

"Look, Beatrice, see how the sails are puffed out to catch the wind from the north."

"Yes, Mother."

"The Nile is an extraordinary waterway. You see, the current flows from south to north, but the prevailing winds usually blow from north to south."

"So what?"

"So people could always travel in either direction—if one needed to go south toward Aswan and Nubia, one simply raised one's sail and sailed there. But if one needed to deliver cargo to the delta and other Mediterranean ports, one simply lowered one's sail and drifted downstream."

"Oh."

"Come along, Bea."

"But, Mother, my feet are tired."

"We're aiming for that bridge right there, right? Straight along now, Beatrice."

Then the plain English words were gone. Maggie looked out across the water. It was true. At full sail, the feluccas blew south. With sails down, the current carried them gently to the north. It was totally opposite from how she always thought of rivers. Whoever heard of water flowing up? Other vessels—barges, passenger ferries, small motorboats, river buses, and sightseeing craft—also moved along the river. A low-slung bridge to her right swept like a stray hair from the eastern bank of downtown to the western bank and the island of Gezira. Over on Gezira, the fronds of the date palm trees blew in the steady breeze.

"Maggie!"

"Hm?"

"Nazaret says it is very strange about the fish."

It is strange, Maggie thought. More strange than even Tareq suspected. These fish were a message from the cats to Maggie. They were a sign, she was sure. But what did the sign mean?

"Oh, my gosh," Maggie said aloud. She had a flash of understanding. The message was so simple and obvious she had to laugh. As easy to understand as the English minutes before. Cats, for heaven's sake! For all their air of mystery they were animals, after all, straightforward and literal. In this message, unlike the messages encoded in hieroglyphs or even the regular old alphabet, sign and meaning were one and the same. Maggie was sure of it. The embassy was targeted for only one reason: something fishy was going on over there.

Chapter 9

The Throne of the Cat

IT WAS NEARLY THREE O'CLOCK by the time Maggie and Tareq got back to the Northern Cemetery. She was ready to collapse. The tomb city was much quieter than it had been the day before. Oum was at work selling poultry and pigeons, and Mr. Zuhayri was visiting with friends at his favorite coffeehouse. Tareq's brothers were scattered around town collecting cast-off articles of clothing from wealthier neighborhoods. The family enclosure was empty,

"My grandmother will soon be home," Tareq said. "She always returns to make a meal for us in the late afternoon so my grandfather does not go hungry to sunset prayers. But if you will sit now I make tea."

"Thanks, Tareq. I have to admit, I am d-dying for something to drink."

Maggie plopped herself down on the freshly swept dirt floor. After pulling off her backpack and resting it on her lap, she leaned back against a low wall and stretched her legs straight out in front of her. Soaked with perspiration, her tee shirt stuck to her back. Inside her sneakers she wiggled her hot toes. She loosened the fabric of her skirt off the raw scrapes on her knee. It still hurt a little from yesterday's fall. She looked over at the small table covered with treasures, then dug out the Bastet figurine.

Tareq returned from filling a carafe with fresh water he got from a spigot out in the alley between enclosures.

"You know, Tareq," Maggie said, "I have to ask you a question. And since we're friends you m-must answer me honestly."

With long nimble fingers Tareq struck a match to the coals in the brazier. Quickly the flames began to heat up the water. He looked at his guest.

"I try."

"Did your grandmother tell you to follow me home yesterday? And did she send you back this morning to follow me today? And if so, w-why?"

"Yesterday my grandmother tell me to see where you live and tell her. I don't know why. But I do what she asks me to do. This morning, I come from my idea alone."

He passed her a small glass of tea. As he extended his arm, Maggie could smell the musky, boyish odor of her friend. It was a new experience being so close to the strong, undeodorized smell of someone her own age. Slow dances in seventh grade and her few awkward hugs with James didn't smell like anything that she could remember except shampoo and potato chips. Certainly not like Tareq.

"Why?"

Maggie sipped the sweet tea and watched Tareq think for a moment. It was evidently hard putting his deepest thoughts and feelings into a language not his own. Like trying to go to bed in a strange place for the first time. You might eventually fall asleep, but it was unlikely that you'd feel completely comfortable, or that you'd sleep well, at least the first night.

"My grandmother says you are special, so I want to see what you do. I want to talk to you. I want to be connected to you to learn what it is like to be you. I want to be not so different from you."

He paused. Maggie nodded. She understood completely. She had asked for an honest answer, but had not expected such a heartfelt reply. Tareq didn't have the will or the words to bend his meaning into a clever response all loaded with sarcasm. There was no *yeah, right.* No eye-rolling *whatever.* What he said came straight from the soul. For Tareq, as for the cats, words and meaning were one and the same.

"I s-see."

"When I saw fish, I knew I could help. Then I knew maybe we could be friends."

"I think we can," Maggie said. "I have an idea that we can help each other. You said Nazaret was a driver for an official. I think I know who you m-mean. I met him yesterday when I was hanging out waiting for my mom. It must be that trade minister guy. And I have a feeling something weird is going on with some American guy named Ramsey but I have no idea w-what. Do you think you could find a way to tag along with Nazaret when he drives?"

"Tag along? What is it to tag?"

Maggie laughed. "S-s-sorry. I mean stay with him. Do what he does when he does it."

Tareq thought a moment. "I have wanted to be driver. Hotels need drivers. Maybe I can ask to learn to driver."

"Learn to b-be a driver like Nazaret. I get it. I wonder. W-well, it can't hurt to ask. If he does say yes, will you try to f-find out everything you can about this situation in Zazazig?"

"I will."

"And Tareq, this will be just be b-between us, right?"

"Between us? Where between us?"

"S-sorry. A figure of speech. You and I will not speak about our arrangement to anyone else, is w-what I'm trying to say."

"I understand."

When Oum arrived a few minutes later Maggie and Tareq were playing a game with six polished stones and a small ram's horn. They were laughing as Maggie tried to make sense of the rules.

"Ah, Maggie!"

Maggie rose to greet Oum, who put down her empty poultry crates and gave her a warm embrace, kissing both her cheeks. When Tareq put away the game, Oum kissed him too. Maggie was a little surprised that Oum did not seem at all surprised to see her.

"I see you children have taken tea," Oum said with approval.

"That's one of the things I like the b-best here," Maggie said. "At home kids don't sit around drinking tea. Soda and juice and sports drinks, and that's about it. And m-milk for younger kids."

"I see," said Oum. She sat down on a stool. Maggie and Tareq sat down at her feet.

As if on cue, four cats padded into the enclosure. One was white, one golden, one black, and one silver striped. Lean with large pointed ears, they circled around the small group and finally approached Maggie. She sat up straight. As usual, her lap formed a scooped hammock just perfect for a cat's resting place. Oum watched the animals as they closed in around Maggie. Which one would settle in the girl's lap and which by her side? Around and around they circled, like moons around Jupiter, like planets around the sun.

The cats meowed as they walked. Their tails, held high, swished back and forth. Their whiskers twitched with electric energy. Maggie's very soul—the center of the orbiting animals—began to vibrate in their presence. She was past the point of wondering what in the world was going on. She was simply present, her senses keenly receiving impressions from one moment to the next. Her breathing grew shallow and quiet. Her palms pressed down on the swept earth. Only her eyes moved, following the circling animals when they passed before her gaze. After three minutes, the white cat finally climbed into her lap and began to knead at the cotton fabric of her skirt. Its front claws dug into the folds and lifted up and down, up and down. Then the cat curled into a ring, nose to tail, and looked up at Maggie's face with orange eyes.

Maggie exhaled. She hesitated to touch the animal before looking at Oum. Oum nodded her approval. Now Maggie stroked the white cat, who closed its eyes and began to purr.

The other cats arranged themselves around Maggie's legs. The silver cat stretched in front of her, the golden cat lay along her right leg, the black cat along her left. They were perfectly symmetrical. Maggie felt the warmth of their bodies pressing against her thighs. What would happen now?

"You are the throne of the white cat," Oum began. "By virtue of your youth and innocence, your freedom from burdens, and your crossing of barriers, the white cat has chosen you. The moon white cat is an escort, a crosser of bridges between worlds. She is there when we are born, and she is there when we die. She keeps us company. From this world to the ancient world, from this time to the old time, from this realm to the sacred realm. My child, the cats are calling upon you for help."

"But why?" Maggie asked. "Why me? And what can I do if I don't kn-know what's wrong?"

"I cannot tell you why they need you right now," Oum said. " I have guesses, but the important thing is you learn on your own. I can tell you where they come from and about how it used to be."

Tareq moved closer to Maggie so that he could pet the black cat as he listened to his grandmother's story. The cats continued to purr.

"In the long ago time," Oum said, "Bastet ruled from her marble halls at Tell Basta. Tell Basta lies in the delta of the mighty Nile along the eastern branch of our life-giving river. The Greeks called the place Bubastis, and Bubastis became the capital of Egypt. The temples of Bubastis were made of gold and marble and polished stone.

"For generations," Oum continued, "the annual festival to celebrate Bastet drew our people from all over Egypt, and even from Nubia and Libya. We came from Kush in the south, from the northern coasts, from the east, and from the western desert. The four points of the compass and the four elements that make us part of life's grand design—earth, air, fire, and water—came together to honor Bastet. There we groomed and prepared our beloved cats, the children of Bastet who had passed from this world, and returned them to her."

Oum stared up into the blue sky beyond Maggie's shoulder. It was as if she were looking at paradise, as if she could recall the festivals from thousands of years ago, as if she, too, had made pilgrimages to Bubastis. Maggie looked down at the cats. Earth, air, fire, and water: there they were. Golden fire, silvery water, black earth, and white air. What was Oum saying? It must be that the four elements in nature each had a color, and those four colors could be seen in the fur of the cat.

"To Bastet the people prayed for release," Oum continued. "They drank beer and prayed for relief from burdens and from suffering. The women clashed their cymbals together, banged their timbrels, raised their skirts to dance. They sang a joyful song. They also told stories of confusions and struggles. The festival turned frenzied, tens of thousands of souls all hungry for relief, a relief which Bastet granted for those hours and days."

Oum looked back at Maggie.

"And in the end, they collapsed. The people went home and sank back into worldly suffering for another year, until next festival."

"Do people still go up to B-bubastis for these festivals?"

Oum lowered her voice and turned bitter. "There are those who do, but only in secret. Our gentle Prophet Mohammed conquered Egypt in year 640, and although he loved cats, our old beliefs were driven underground and behind the veil. Since then the *ka* of Bastet has been dormant. What you would call asleep."

The strange syllable reminded Maggie of what she'd wanted to ask Oum the last time.

"But w-what is this *ka* and *ba,* Oum? I heard you s-s-say those words last time we met, but I still don't really understand what they mean."

Oum looked as though she were trying to locate a suitable place to begin her answer.

"Our ancestors believed in something called *maat. Maat* described what you might call 'the right order.' In the right order, the vital forces of creation are all as they should be. Not necessarily peaceful—for we know that there is always strife and unpleasantness in the world. Right order means that those who must battle are battling, and that each element of creation is playing its particular role. Do you follow me so far?"

"Yes, I think so."

"Now think about all the forms of life on earth—every person, every plant, every animal, every insect. *Ba* is the individual spirit within all living things. Western people call *ba* the soul. *Ka* is much larger. *Ka* is eternal vital force, a universal power that exists everywhere and all the time."

Maggie was lost again. She decided to let it go for now.

Oum's hand clasped the place under her chin where her flowered blue scarf was pinned. Maggie thought she detected a note of resentment in Oum's voice.

"There is no longer *maat* in my country," Oum went on. "Bubastis is no more the place it was. It is a different place. There still remain the catacombs where the spirits of the sacred cats rise from their mummified bodies. In Bubastis there is an Old Kingdom chapel, but it is now crumbled to ruins. The catabombs can be entered, but..."

"But w-what?"

Oum looked directly into Maggie's green eyes.

"Those whose memories have been betrayed do not look kindly on intrusion."

Maggie shivered.

"What do you m-mean 'betrayed'?"

Now Oum was almost angry.

"Look around you. Look at us! We are poor. We are too many poor people. Bastet once promised us fertility and abundance and the fulfillment of our human desires. Well, if this is the fulfillment of our human desires—people crushing one upon the other and living among the souls of our dead—then I no longer want to be human. I'd rather be a river rat. No, this is not fulfillment. This is feral human existence. It is not what Bastet wants for us. We sacrificed to her for centuries. We honored her. But her spirit has been sleeping, sleeping through our misery. Until now. Now the spirit of Bastet is...is..."

"Is w-what?" Maggie was trying hard to follow, but Oum's feelings were shifting from dreamy hope, to scorn, to rage, and finally to disbelief. It was hard to know what to think. Oum seemed so upset, and Maggie was lost in the words. Maybe pretending not to speak English and then speaking so much at once was what made Oum's explanation so baffling. Obviously, lots of things about Egypt were pretty messed up. But something more than Maggie's question had triggered Oum's outburst. Maggie was totally in the dark.

Oum remained silent, staring at the hundreds of tombs behind Maggie's shoulder.

"Is w-what?" Maggie repeated in a whisper. With her right hand Maggie continued to pet the smooth hair of the white cat in her lap.

"Oum?" Maggie tried another way.

"Yes?"

"You said Bubastis is not a place anymore. But that people s-still go there. What's it called if it's not called B-Bubastis?"

Even Tareq, who was doing his best to follow, turned to his grandmother with curiosity.

"The sacred halls of the temple of Bastet remain in Bubastis, but the dark passages that wind for a mile underground, and in which the *ka* of Bastet has lain dormant for centuries among the remains of her children, each one lovingly prepared for the next world, are under a delta town that you can see on any map of Egypt today. The name of the town is Zagazig."

"Zagazig?" Maggie said, remembering the place that had everything to do with her mother's work here in Cairo. "There's some sort of cotton factory there, I think. Where some kind of b-business deal is happening. A guy called Ramsey wants to expand the factory. But what if his expansion p-penetrates the catacombs of Bastet?"

Oum gripped Maggie by the shoulders.

"Do you now see, daughter? Do you now see why I cried out when I heard this right here in my home from the lips of your father?"

Maggie recalled Oum's extreme reaction, which she hadn't understood at the time. Now it all made more sense. If there were real cats buried in Zagazig, and if the guardian spirit of Bastet were disrupted, what might happen? Ramsey's construction project could lead to disaster. Maggie's hand left the back of the purring white cat and drew out the Bastet figurine. As usual, it warmed to her touch. Maggie looked straight into Oum's eyes and spoke from her heart.

"I think I am b-beginning to understand you, Oum."

Oum released Maggie's shoulders and rose to assemble her cooking supplies. Maggie spoke quietly to Tareq.

"Tareq, didn't you say Nazaret was driving the m-minister again tonight? I think we ought to make sure you can be there, too. Tell Nazaret whatever you need to tell him, but try to learn what you can. I have got to know what's going on around here."

Chapter 10
Accommodations

SHAWQUI MAHFOUZ SAT OUTSIDE on his terrace. The minister lived in a plush residential block on the island of Zamalek. His housecat, a blue-gray Persian called Pasha, lay curled in a contented ball under the table. From a small white china cup trimmed with gold the minister sipped a late afternoon demitasse of espresso. A sheaf of papers lay stacked neatly on the table. As he read, he laid page after page of the document face down inside a dossier. Every so often he put down his silver pen and pushed his spectacles further up the bridge of his nose. Then he resumed jotting notes into his leather-bound daily notebook. He stopped writing when he heard a timid knock followed by a stronger one. Inside the apartment his houseman opened the front door. Minutes later, to the minister's surprise, Nazaret was standing on the terrace with a rather unkempt boy at his side.

"Well, now," he said. "Who is this?"

"This is a boy called Tareq, Excellency." Nazaret smiled. "He is a friend."

"A friend," the minister repeated, looking over the barefoot visitor. He knew that Nazaret would not have brought Tareq without a reason, Still, to the minister he looked like any other Egyptian boy of the street.

"I am showing him the ways of the driver," Nazaret said. "He wants to learn. He wants to be ready to work when his time comes."

"Admirable," said the minister. Unable to meet the minister's direct gaze, Tareq looked down at the floor.

"Nazaret," the minister said. "Have you any idea how many American farmers grow cotton?"

"No, Excellency."

The minister pushed himself away from the table. "Twenty-five thousand farmers," he said. "And every one of these farmers possesses roughly one million dollars' worth of money and assets. Adding to their personal wealth, the American government pays these cotton farmers four and a half billion dollars in cash every single year to grow their cotton. With this extra cash in hand, the farmers can sell their cotton for less money than it takes to grow it. What were the numbers?"

The minister leaned forward to glance at his notes.

"Oh, yes: growing a pound of cotton costs the American farmer 73 cents. But government contributes a subsidy of more than 40 cents a pound. That means that the American farmer can afford to sell cotton for the going world price of 35 cents a pound. Thirty-five cents a pound!"

The minister shook his head in disbelief. "Are you following this, Tareq? Fully half of their true cost of production. Even this child selling tangerines in the street knows that if it costs him three *piastres* to acquire each tangerine and he sells them for one *piastre* apiece, he is going to lose money. Unless..."

The minister's voice turned bitter.

"Unless his Papa gives him extra money to begin with, an unfair advantage over the other children hawking on the same street. Wouldn't you agree? Wouldn't you agree, Tareq?"

"I agree, sir," Tareq said, shifting his weight from one leg to the other.

"No," said Minister Mahfouz, pressing his thumb crisply down onto the ledge of his mother-of-pearl lighter and lighting himself a cigarette. "We Egyptians can produce our cotton for 50 cents a pound, but we just can't compete with people who are spoon-fed their profits from their own government before ever engaging the world market.

"No wonder Moussa got me these papers so urgently yesterday afternoon. And no wonder Ramsey doesn't discuss the benefits he reaps from his government subsidies. It would make him look like a charity case, a welfare case. Naturally we would wonder: why should we go into business with a foreigner on the dole? Would you, Nazaret? Would you give a felucca ride to a tourist who didn't have the money to pay you when the ride was over?"

"That depends, Excellency. But probably not."

"Well. Why should a government do what a single man will not do?" The question was rhetorical; the minister had posed this question to himself eight times already in the last hour. He exhaled cigarette smoke in a thin blue stream.

"I'll tell you why. Because we are poor. Because we are hungry. Because we need work. Because if we don't do something to lift our people from misery, the fundamental Islamists will continue to draw upon our young men like this boy here and drive them to vengeful, self-destructive jihad. Because with the world price of cotton plunging, we cannot compete directly with the cotton growers in the United States. No matter how little we pay our laborers, we cannot get production costs lower than 50 cents a pound, or harvest more than one ton of cotton off an acre of land. Because we might as well benefit from the largesse of the American taxpayer, who underwrites the cotton industry. Because if you cannot beat the bully, Nazaret, you join sides with him. Another playground lesson, at least for the morally weak. Isn't this so, Tareq?"

Tareq said nothing. Nazaret replied instead.

"Is Egypt now to be morally weak, Excellency?"

The minister raised his voice.

"How moral can someone be when they are hungry, Nazaret? I ask you this man to man. How moral is the man who starves?"

Nazaret looked down, frowned, and fell silent. The sun dipped closer to the western desert. Pasha closed his eyes and fell asleep at the minister's feet. Tareq looked at Nazaret, waiting for some cue about what to do with himself. His bare feet were not accustomed to the cool smoothness of the parquet floor. After some minutes, Nazaret cleared his throat and spoke.

"The boy and I will be downstairs waiting in the car, Excellency. We will leave for the evening's affair at six o'clock."

"Thank you, Nazaret," the minister said without looking up.

Downstairs, Nazaret and Tareq waited in the early evening breeze. When Minister Mahfouz joined them a few minutes later, he appeared to have put the disturbing conversation out of his mind, at least for the time being. He patted Tareq on the shoulder before ducking into the back seat of the heavy sedan. Nazaret swung the door closed and motioned Tareq to get in the passenger side of the front seat. Once in motion, Nazaret addressed the figure in the rear view mirror.

"Excellency, my friend Tareq brought a young visitor down to the boat this morning."

"Oh?"

"I believe she is the daughter of the American lady attaché whom you met."

The minister recalled the tidy official in the dingy office.

"Elizabeth McKee?"

"That's right, sir."

The minister reflected for a few minutes. "Was she also with her mother?"

"No, Excellency."

"Alone then with Tareq?"

"Yes, sir."

It was not Nazaret's place to draw conclusions and spread information he picked up on the street. But if the minister speculated, Nazaret might confirm or deny those speculations. The minister's relationship with Nazaret was one reason the minister seemed not to have lost touch—as had many other officials—with what it was like to be a regular Egyptian trying to get by.

Tareq filed away these insights to tell Maggie later.

Nazaret leaned on his horn. He was trying to get past a peddler blocking an intersection. The peddler's donkey was loaded with baskets of double-A batteries still in their transparent but impenetrable packaging. The donkey laid back its ears and shambled out of the way.

"This boy's people, Nazaret. Who are they?"

"I know Tareq's family well," the driver said. "The grandfather I know from the coffeehouse. An honorable and old family, very devout Muslims, but poor. Their apartment building collapsed in the 1992 earthquake. Since that time they have lived in the Northern Cemetery in the family tomb. The boy's father left Cairo for Saudi Arabia but has not yet returned. The mother died in the collapse. An odd friend for this girl of the attaché, but a good boy. He helps me out sometimes on my felucca and I pay him. Now he is learning what it means to be a driver."

"I see."

Tareq noticed that Nazaret didn't say anything to his employer about the dead fish.

Maggie arrived back at the apartment at exactly a quarter to five, right on time. She went straight to the back hall by the mailboxes to check the kittens. The mother cat was gone. Maggie picked up the black one and tucked it under her chin. After petting it for a minute or two she put it down and fondled the other two, one at a time. The white one licked her face with a dry, rough tongue.

After murmuring a quick goodbye, Maggie let herself into the apartment and found her parents moving at full tilt. The apartment was steamy from the shower, the air clouded with her mother's perfume and her father's after shave. Standing in a half slip and bra, her mother was leaning forward over the bathroom sink applying makeup; Paul was trying to see his image in the living room window in order to straighten his tie.

"What's going on? W-where are you guys off to?"

Elizabeth didn't put down her mascara wand.

"Cocktail party. A no-brainer but a command performance. Baumsdorfer will be there, and the ambassador. The usual suspects. Hey, thank you for being on time, Mag. How was your day?"

"I'll tell you all about it, but first you tell me w-what's up. Am I s-supposed to come to this thing? I'm totally exhausted."

"Your dad and I have to go for a couple of hours. But you don't. It won't be late, though. Just drinks at the Egyptian Museum. If you have a snack now we can all eat when we get back around eight."

"W-what's the party for?" Maggie plopped down on the couch. She draped one long leg over the back of the sofa and put an arm behind her neck.

"Something in honor of a new French official," Elizabeth replied. "All the embassy people have to go. This guy I'm working with, Ramsey, is going to be there too, since he's here on that Zagazig business. Which means I'm in charge of keeping him company and showing him around."

Maggie's ears startled at the Z word. Zagazig! She jumped to her feet.

"Can I come w-with you guys?"

Elizabeth was back at the bathroom sink.

"Oh, honey, you'll be bored to tears. Lots of shaking hands and meeting people, then smiling and standing around making small talk. Exactly what you hate."

"Actually," Paul said, giving his tie a firm yank. "It's exactly what *you* hate, Elizabeth."

"I'd s-still like to go," Maggie said, ignoring her dad's crack. "Please? I can be ready in ten m-minutes."

Paul gave her the nod and she nipped off to the shower. He spoke to his wife.

"Think about it. That place is always jammed with tourists and visitors. Even if she spends some time meeting and greeting, she'll still get to see things that we haven't been able to see on our own because of the crowds."

"I guess so." Elizabeth stepped into a sleeveless black dress and wiggled it into position. She presented her back to her husband to be zipped. Then she put on a fitted black long-sleeved jacket with silver buttons. "But now we won't have an excuse to get out of there early."

By six o'clock Maggie and her parents were walking toward Al-Azhar, the largest thoroughfare in their neighborhood. They passed several large buses crammed with tourists on their way to the bustling Khan al-Khalili bazaar. On Al-Azhar Paul stopped to hail a taxi.

"The Egyptian Museum, please."

Maggie and her mother scooted across the hot sticky vinyl of the back seat.

The driver, with a half-smoked unfiltered cigarette dangling from his lower lip, nodded. "Al-Mathaf, yes, the museum."

Maggie sat roasting. It was the first time in many days she had not pulled her hair straight back into a pony tail. She had blown it dry, and now the back of her neck was beginning to perspire.

The taxi pulled up to the museum. Easing herself gently over the seat, Maggie unstuck her thighs from the hot vinyl and stepped onto the curb. She smoothed her skirt down her legs and shouldered her tiny purse. It contained two dozen Egyptian pounds, her passport, and the Bastet figurine. Maggie no longer went anywhere without the bronze cat.

A black sedan with privacy windows pulled up behind their taxi. While her father paid the fare, Maggie had a chance to observe who got out of the car.

"Excellency!" Elizabeth said.

Minister Mahfouz took her hand. "A pleasure, Elizabeth." He looked at Maggie.

"I think you may remember meeting my daughter, Margaret Underwood."

Maggie smiled and shook his hand. The skin was smooth and moist, as if he'd just applied lotion.

"Hello, Margaret, it is a pleasure to meet you again so soon."

"Hello," Maggie said. She looked at the driver, too, who was standing by the back door of the car. He nodded his head to her. She smiled at Nazaret. Then she saw Tareq half hiding by the passenger side. He gave a small nod and Maggie nodded back. That was a good sign. It meant that he might have learned something about the project in Zagazig. But Maggie was careful not to call attention to Tareq right now.

After Maggie's father and Minister Mahfouz exchanged formal greetings, Elizabeth and the Egyptian walked off together toward the museum entrance. Paul took Maggie's arm. She looked back and waved bye to Nazaret and Tareq.

The sky had darkened to a shade of blue that made the pinkish stone of the museum practically glow. In front of the building was a grassy garden filled with statues, stone sculptures, palm trees, and a small version of the sphinx. The entrance to the building itself was an ornately carved bronze door situated within a giant panel of sculpted marble. The doorway looked about four stories tall, and was flanked by two equally tall white columns that supported an arch. The shape of the huge white arch was echoed in immense windows that ran east and west from the front door. Paul whistled.

"This is some neo-classical structure."

"Come on, D-dad. I agree it's pretty, but does it have to have a label?"

"As a matter of fact, yes," he said. "And I hope you see the connection. The architect very deliberately designed this place, which was going to house the treasures of one ancient civilization—Egypt's—in the aesthetic style of another ancient civilization—Greece. Both are civilizations we call classical."

"It's like what you were saying about the p-pyramid on the dollar bill," Maggie said.

"Exactly. Art's all about paying your respects, if you know what I mean."

"I know what you mean. At least, I think I know what you mean. You have to refer to what's already b-been done."

"Exactly. If not openly, then implicitly. Nobody works in a vacuum."

On the front steps a string quartet was playing Debussy. For several minutes, as guests gathered by the entrance, the harmonious sound of the violins and cellos was drowned out by the sundown call to prayer. Maggie was getting used to these cross-cultural moments—an American party honoring French tradition in an Egyptian setting.

Maggie watched the well-heeled Cairenes stroll into the party. Women in long rustling dresses of sapphire and emerald, men in black suits. Jewels sparkled on hands, lips were painted red, and silk handkerchiefs were folded in perfect shapes that stood out from front pockets. Many of the Egyptian men were wearing pale blue or red *galabiyyas,* more formal versions of the simple cotton caftan Mr. Zuhayri wore. Delicate embroidery in golden threads decorated the front of these long tunics.

Passing into the cool dark front chamber of the hundred-year-old museum, Maggie felt practically royal.

Paul gave her hand a squeeze. "I see a bar over there if you want a Coke. People are passing hors d'oeuvres. Help yourself. But I better get over to mom and play husband."

Maggie was glad that her mother had been swept into her official role. Now it would be easier to wander around on her own and see if she could lay eyes on Bill Ramsey. She'd only seen him once when he was in the conference room on the other side of that thin partition. And that had only been a reflection. Would she recognize him again?

A large crowd was mingling at the bar, so Maggie decided to wait a while for a drink. She was famished and immediately looked for a waiter passing something. When a white-gloved servant cruised along bearing a silver tray, she made a bee line in his direction.

"Mademoiselle?"

Maggie took a cocktail napkin off the tray and helped herself to four small puff pastries which turned out to be stuffed with a kind of cheese she loved. Hors d'oeuvres in hand, she crossed the marble floor to a wooden bench up against a rack of brochures. She sat down and started eating. It was delicious. The Gruyère cheese was warm and the pastry crust melted in her mouth. Then again, she thought, she must have walked a thousand miles today. Just about anything would have tasted ambrosial. Maggie put the other cheese puffs down on the napkin and reached for a brochure. This place is immense, Maggie thought, studying the map and layout. More than 120,000 relics on display. But what caught her eye was the description of the contents of Room 54.

Animal mummies.

Chapter 11

"I Am MAU"

The few bites of warm melted cheese made Maggie realize how hungry she was. Before she could go view the animal mummies, she just had to have something else to eat. Still, she didn't want to get caught up in any social mingling. Fortunately, large wood and glass display cases stood in the atrium where the party-goers were chatting in groups. Maybe she could get another handful of appetizers and eat them behind a display case. She'd have to be discreet. Maggie sidled over to a servant bearing a fully loaded tray.

With five more cheese puffs and a glass of icy Sprite, Maggie retreated to a position behind the glass of an unlit case. The tall dusty unit contained unlabeled statuettes of various pharoahs in standing and sitting positions. Just as Cairo was filled to bursting with people, so this museum was stuffed with artifacts torn from tombs, rubble, and the river bed. On every shelf in front of her the nameless statuettes stood shoulder to shoulder. She sat down cross-legged on the cool marble and listened to the formal speeches of gratitude and welcome made by the officials at the party. What a relief to be by herself and out of sight.

After the speeches, Maggie heard footsteps approach the other side of the tall cabinet. Two sets of footsteps. She swallowed and stayed quiet.

She heard an American voice with a southern accent. It was an effort for the voice to speak softly, which made it easier for Maggie to hear what it said.

"I'm told that you are the man I need to see," the voice said.

There was no reply. Maggie assumed the other person assented in silence.

"I'm also told that a man cannot be too careful here, particularly an American man. But we both come from courteous backgrounds, so I might ask you in a courteous manner: Do you mind, sir, if I ask you to show me some identification. I understand that in your possession is the other half of the broken object I am holding right here in my pocket. Can you present me with this object or can you not?"

The voice dripped with condescension thinly masked by a twist of humor. Maggie recognized it as Ramsey's. Every single instinct told her to shrink away, to make herself small, to listen in absolute silence. She wondered if the second man had what Ramsey wanted. The next words answered her question.

"Well, then, sir, it looks to me like we are going to proceed with our transaction. Doubling the size of our joint and mutually beneficial operations here begins next month. Assuming the demolition and construction moves right along, I will need the next delivery of—"

The voice made a low, sinister sound that Maggie knew was intended to be a chuckle but sounded more like a growl.

"—goods, shall we say, that y'all will provide, in place and ready for operation, in a period of no more than six months."

The other person was determined, it seemed to Maggie, never to speak aloud. But the man must have nodded, because Ramsey was pleased.

"Good. I expect to see that your reputation as an honorable businessman is founded in practice. There's lots more—benefits, shall we say?—that could end up paddin' the right places of your wallet, if you catch my drift. A man such as myself, who is taking a chance so far from home on this venture—much to the chagrin of some members of my own family, I have to admit—can rely only on the most dependable of suppliers. They tell me that your goods always come from the finest stock, the most hardy of raw materials. As we southerners say, give me a young, able-bodied boy and I will give you the world."

The odd emphasis Ramsey placed on his words made Maggie's scalp prickle. It was like he was talking about something by translating it into another language, a language meant to cloud, not clarify, his meaning. It reminded her of the days when her parents had to talk about something important in her presence, something that they didn't want her to know about but couldn't put off discussing. She used to get frustrated with them. But this was different. This was horrifying.

Ramsey must have handed the other man some money, because he went on.

"Please do your counting in a discreet location, sir. I think you will find that I have covered your expenses as detailed in the offer you tendered to me last summer. If you find anything at all amiss, you do know that you can reach me for the next few days at the Sheraton. You know the one, the Gesundheit, or Gazebo, or Gazeebra, or some such thing over on the island. And now, if you'll pardon me, I must get back in to the swim of this lovely get-together. The French ambassador has the most adorable executive assistant with whom I was engaged in a very interesting conversation."

Maggie could barely breathe. Sitting on the floor with her knees raised, she pressed her head against her kneecaps and wrapped her arms around her shins. She remained in this balled-up position until she was sure the men were gone. Then she heard another voice, this time inside her own head.

Maggie reached for her shoulder bag and unfastened the brass clasp.

She pulled out the figurine, and wasn't surprised to find it burning hot. Perhaps because she was expecting the heat, her fingers didn't recoil this time. She passed Bastet from hand to hand slowly and thought about what she had just heard. There were so many questions. First, what was the object the two men had reassembled in order for the conversation to have taken place? She would have given anything to see that. And then, who was that other guy? He never said a word, so Maggie had no idea whether he was American, Egyptian, French, or from some other place. No, wait, she did. Ramsey had said something about courteous backgrounds. But no, that didn't help. The French had just as much pride in their courtesy as the Egyptians. She had heard her mother talk about the polite manners of the French about a million times. For that matter, the man could have been Japanese or Afghani, Italian or English—many cultures prided themselves on courtesy. And what were the "goods" the man had referred to? It seemed crazy, but Ramsey's insinuations made her think they were boys. Could people actually bargain with kids as if they were things? Such a strange and creepy deal. The one and only thing she knew for sure was that Bill Ramsey, the guy planning the expansion in Zagazig—in Bubastis—was up to something troubling and secret.

Maggie wasn't sure what she ought to do. Maybe Bastet would guide her next move. But the figurine had cooled. It was up to Maggie. She decided to stick to her original plan and go find the animal mummies. She returned the figurine to her shoulder bag and got up. Her legs were stiff from being in a tense ball for so long. Maggie stretched them out and looked around for the best way to go upstairs. She didn't want to double back through the middle of the party. Looking into the darkened rear of the ground floor, Maggie knew there must be a stairwell at the north end of the building. Sure enough, there was a sign.

She passed the gallery where King Tutankhamen's famous solid gold death mask was displayed. This was exactly the sort of famous object her dad wanted to see during the museum's off-hours. Oh, well. It wasn't going to be tonight. She had an entirely different agenda. Maggie turned left and went through a room full of gilded wooden shrines of graduated size. On the sides of the sarcophagi Maggie saw hippos, cows, and cats—lots of cats.

Once past the shrines Maggie sped from a walk to a run. Now she raced past a room full of scarabs. Arriving at the northwest stairway, she leaped up the well-worn marble steps two at a time. She checked the walls for signs to Room 54. Her hunt led her full speed back down the long dark north-to-south corridor of the second floor of the museum. She screeched to a stop at the corner, turned left, and ran until she arrived outside Room 54. It was just above the ground floor museum entrance.

Maggie stepped slowly into the dark musty chamber. She was still panting from the dash down the hall. She stood for a moment to let her breath return to normal. She drew Bastet from her shoulder bag, kissed the figurine, and held it tightly in her left hand. Dimming daylight filtered through the small circles of stained glass windows. Maggie could barely see. As if by a magnetic force, she was drawn slowly to a particular display around which dim dusty sunbeams swirled. She dropped to her knees. Maggie placed her free hand on the glass as if she could reach through and give comfort to what lay inside.

Behind the smudged glass was a dark, dessicated lump: the mummified remains of a cat. The tail was a brittle black string, the hair on the ear points spiky like cactus bristles. The body was caved in upon itself like an empty leather glove. All the protective layers of linen had been peeled off, exposing the mummy to curators and tourists. Beside the cat was a milk-colored jar containing its preserved vital organs. The top of the jar was formed into the face of Bastet. On a label affixed to the glass Maggie read a description of the remains before her.

> **CAT MUMMY**
> **Retrieved from Bubasteion in 1923. Found in the tomb of Zphardikia.**
> **Archaeologists believe that Zphardikia was the wife of the pharoah's royal gardener, Hemphat.**

Maggie's eyes filled with tears. So, Maggie thought, this animal had belonged to a living, breathing person. Someone who had a name. A woman with a name. Zphardikia had been buried with her cat, a cat that was meant to keep her company in the next world. Maybe Zphardikia's cat had chased butterflies in the pharoah's garden. Maybe he liked to bask in the sun under the stroking hand of the gardener's wife. Maybe he earned his keep by killing the rodents that spoiled the stores of grain. Some tomb raider had not only dug it up, but had unwrapped its protective linen and exposed it to the eyes of the ages. This seemed so wrong to Maggie she was speechless. When Maggie finally spoke, her voice was a whisper. "It's okay," she said. "I'm here now."

In the silence of Room 54, she heard another voice coming from the doorway behind her.

"MAU."

Maggie jumped up.

In the dusky doorway she saw an image, a small wavy figure that was both present and not present. With her free hand Maggie wiped her eyes to be sure she was seeing what she thought she was seeing. Shimmering on the threshhold was her own cat, Sarah. Maggie heard the cat's voice and saw her as plain as could be. Yet she wasn't solid, she was shimmering the way a reflection on the surface of water shimmered under a breeze.

"Sarah?"

This time she saw the cat's mouth move as it gave voice three times to Maggie's name, or rather, to the other form of her name.

"MAU. MAU. MAU."

"Sarah, I'm right here."

Maggie wanted to approach, but something anchored her in place. With her left hand she brought the figurine to her heart and held it there. She put her other hand on the glass of the case behind her. And while she waited for a sign, her gaze locked upon the great green eyes of the spirit cat on the threshold. Things were beginning to seem connected. Slowly, as if her arm were moving through the viscous mud of the flooding Nile, she moved the figurine from her heart to her forehead. Maggie spoke as if in a trance.

"From my heart's thought to my tongue's command, I know who I am: I am *MAU.*"

Chapter 12

In the Dark

SARAH'S IMAGE VANISHED and the spell was broken.

Maggie ran full speed back down to the museum's main atrium. She felt like something huge had happened, something that made her bigger and better than she had been just moments before. Back at the party, she snaked through the knots of chatting people until she found her mother standing with three others. Breathless and flushed, Maggie figured she must have looked pretty disheveled. Her mom's eyes widened at the sight of her.

"Maggie," Elizabeth said. "You know Minister Mahfouz. And this is Mr. Baumsdorfer, from our State Department.

"Hello," Maggie said to the American. She shook his hand. His moist hand went limp in hers, as if he didn't really think she merited a real shake.

"And this is Monsieur DuCompte."

Maggie extended her hand again. She felt like showing off. "*Bon soir,*" she said. "*Comment-allez vous*?"

The Frenchman smiled and shook her hand. "*Très bien, Mademoiselle. Alors je trouve que vous avez l'ésprit diplomâtique comme votre mère.*"

Maggie felt proud that he had compared her to her mother; not knowing the words to thank him properly, she accepted the compliment with a smile. Then she mustered a bit more French to apologize for her limited vocabulary. *"Je m'éxcuse, mais je ne parle pas beaucoup de français, monsieur.*"

"*Ça ne fait rien,*" said Monsieur DuCompte. "*Vous essayez, et celá toujours suffit.*"

Maggie continued to smile at his gracious comment as Elizabeth excused herself and Maggie from the two men with a handshake and one last pleasantry. Then her mother bent close.

"You must be ravenous," she said. "I'll just tell Mr. Ramsey that we're going and we'll see if we can find your father." Elizabeth scanned the crowd. "Oh, there's Bill." She caught his eye and waved. Ramsey approached.

"Why, Lizzie honey, don't tell me that this grown up lovely lady is your daughter. You can't possibly be old enough to have a child this age."

Disgusted by the voice she was growing to loathe, Maggie dutifully extended her hand for the third time. Ramsey clasped it in both of his and held on. Maggie hated when people did that. She especially hated it now.

"Yes, Bill. This is my daughter, Margaret Underwood. Maggie, this is William Ramsey. Mr. Ramsey is in Cairo working on a business project in Zagazig."

If Ramsey didn't let go of her hand this instant, Maggie thought she might scream. After what had just happened upstairs, coming face to face with this man was more than she could tolerate. As the big blockhead grinned down at her, Maggie felt a furious heat pounding outward from her heart into her head and limbs. She was taken by surprise when Ramsey actually tossed her hand away as if it had burned him.

"Little lady, I believe you might be runnin' a fever," he said. "You downright scorched this tough old paw of mine."

Maggie said nothing. She muttered something about feeling fine and tried to figure out what had just happened.

The cab ride home was quiet. Maggie looked out the window and mulled over the evening's strange events.

"By the way, honey," her mom said, stirring Maggie out of her thoughts. "Mr. Vance wrote back to you. He says fine about the cat essay, and that you should go for it. He did remind you to keep track of your sources, though. He'll need to see a bibliography."

Maggie was amused. Would Oum's stories count as a reference? How would a person cite *her* as a source? Not to mention the unspoken voice of Bastet communicating with her, or the cats whose messages started with the rotting bodies of dead fish.

"That's great," she said yawning. She put her head against the window in the back seat as the neon lights of downtown flashed by in a blur. "Thanks for checking."

Maggie was going to have to think again about this project. How could *All the Cats of Cairo* be an informative essay and also reflect what she was now sure were supernatural influences? It was going to have to be a description of the real live cats, and a record of her experience communicating with a sacred being. Well, she had to begin somewhere. At home she got started.

I'm not sure I can figure any of this out. Maybe I ought to begin with what I know. The Bastet figurine is using heat to communicate with me. It happened at Oum's. It happened when Ramsey talked about digging up the foundation for that cotton factory expansion. If the figurine of Bastet is trying to get through to me this way, that means that the goddess herself is, too. And now at least some of her power has been transferred to me. I'm almost sure that what Ramsey felt in my hand was the heat I feel in the figurine. But what is he doing, exactly? All I know is that something is so messed up that Bastet has called me. Bastet and the other cats, too. All of them. Even the poor cat in the museum, dead for so long. And Sarah. And the cat in the hall. And Oum's calico cat. And the ones by the obelisk, the obelisk where I first saw the name MAU. But how can I use the powers I've been given if I don't understand what's wrong?

But back to real cat stories. I read the other day that even Mohammed loved cats, which I think is interesting since Oum seems pretty mad about some of the Muslim traditions. One time when Mohammed was meditating this cat came over and fell asleep on the sleeve of his tunic. When it was time to go, Mohammmed didn't want to disturb her so instead of waking her up he cut off his sleeve.

Maggie stopped writing and looked up from the page. Her left hand was cramped from writing so much so fast. She cracked her knuckles. Maggie knew the problem at Zagazig/Bubastis wasn't something she could share with her parents, at least not yet. She wasn't ready to share the sense she had of her mission, especially when she didn't understand what her mission was all about. After all, her mother was actually working with that awful Ramsey. Maggie twirled her hair and tallied up some of the incidents she'd need to record in more detail. The dead fish, the cats of Heliopolis, the kittens in the hall, the figurine in her pocket, the four different cats that came to her at Oum's, the vision of Sarah. Maggie shivered at the memory of the black and shriveled carcass of the exposed cat mummy. Once upon a time that cat had been alive and warm. Once upon a time someone had held that cat in her arms. And once upon a time, when that cat had died, someone had carefully and ceremonially embalmed its body and provided it with what it needed to live in the afterlife. Once upon a time that cat had been treated as a sacred being. Now it was unearthed and utterly exposed, collecting dust behind glass in a museum. Maggie couldn't help it. She started to cry. She knew she was tired. She knew she was hungry. But she also knew she had to do something. Maybe writing everything down would eventually make things clearer. What was Mr. Vance always saying? If you can't write it, then you don't know it.

Maggie was quiet all through dinner. Afterward she cleared the table and washed the dishes. By then she was so tired she could barely speak. She changed into a tee shirt and pajama bottoms.

She got under the covers and looked up at the ceiling. Tonight her bedtime game took on a new meaning.

Above her head was Bubastis, a land ruled by cats. The queen of Bubastis was Bastet, whose reign guaranteed joy and abundance for all of Nature's creation. Bastet's servant was MAU, Maggie herself, only in a different form. Sleepily, Maggie envisioned herself as handmaiden to the magical cat goddess. MAU saw that the queen was kept brushed and stroked. MAU reported disharmonies in the land. Under Bastet's rule the cats always had plenty of good hunting at sunset, and cool running water to drink at noon. When thirsty, the cats would lean out over clear rivulets that trickled over clean gray rocks. The kittens leaped from stone to stone in the middle of the streams. Under the waxing moon the females walked silently through meadows pocked with rodent holes. In the light of day, solitary old males lay on warm exposed places, their faces turned to the sun.

Chapter 13

Getting Familiar

MAGGIE SLEPT FOR twelve hours. When she opened her eyes it was nearly ten. Wide awake, she lay unmoving in bed for several minutes. She heard clattering sounds from the kitchen and smelled bacon. Sunday morning. Cairo. She got up and went into the living room. Her parents, lounging in sweats and tee shirts themselves, greeted her with relief.

"That was some sleep," Paul said.

"You were wiped out," said her mother. "I think taking you to that party was a mistake."

"No, I was just totally exhausted by the time we got home. Tareq and I walked for miles yesterday. I'm sorry if I was rude to that guy you're working with."

"I don't think he could tell," Elizabeth said, pouring a glass of mango juice.

Maggie sat down at the table and drank some juice. She buttered a warm circle of pita bread, spread a large dollop of orange marmalade on top, and lay two pieces of bacon across the jelly. She folded it over and took a big bite.

"Mmm. You know," she said when she had swallowed a couple of mouthfuls, "I was wondering. Are you planning to go out to Zagazig any time soon? You know, to check out this cotton factory?"

"Probably not until the groundbreaking on Tuesday. Why?"

"Could I come along?"

"I'll have to check on that. I can't say for certain."

Maggie took another sip of juice. "Mom?"

"Hm?"

"What do you think of Bill Ramsey?"

Elizabeth put down the newspaper.

"Well, if you mean do I think he wants to do business here, I think, yes, that's exactly what he wants to do. And I think that his doing business here is a good thing. At least, I hope it is."

"But you're paid to hope it is. No offense or anything, but you have to help a person in his position."

Elizabeth looked at her daughter's serious face. Maggie had never taken much interest in Elizabeth's bureaucratic paper-shuffling in D.C.

"If you're asking me do I like the man, then I can tell you the truth—as long as the truth doesn't leave this room."

Maggie swore.

"Bill Ramsey is exactly the kind of man I hate, Maggie."

"I thought we didn't use the word hate in this family."

"You're right. Bill Ramsey is exactly the kind of man I dislike intensely. I prefer people who speak directly in plain English."

Maggie knew what her mother meant. The smiling, the flattery, the flowery speech—all of that showy sporty way of trying to get admired was exactly what she, too, hated about the way some boys in her class behaved. But the boys her age were obviously just trying to get in with the popular crowd. It was easier for some boys to goof around and make people laugh than to make a reputation for themselves as students or athletes. That's why she'd liked James. He didn't let himself get pushed into a category. He wasn't a super jock. He wasn't a Type-A student. He wasn't a nerd. He wasn't a prep. He certainly was not Goth. He was just himself. Maybe a little naïve and goofy. But he was nice. He thought about stuff. He was a good friend. And he was definitely not a class clown. A person like Bill Ramsey was grown up. Shouldn't he have grown out of clowning? What was he trying to get all the time? She was sure that Ramsey's plan had something to do with the fishiness at the embassy. Something also to do with getting boys to work for him. And all of this, everything he planned to do at Zagazig was enraging all the cats of Cairo. Only Maggie—and maybe Oum—knew this to be true. But now wasn't the time to share her insights with her mother.

"Then how can you trust him to do what he says he's going to do?"

Elizabeth took a sip of tea.

"I don't have to trust him, honey. As you might put it, I'm not paid to trust him. I'm just paid to make him sit down with the people here and sign what he needs to sign to make the project move forward. If he fails to do what he has signed his name to doing, someone else is paid to deal with the consequences of that. Although it goes without saying that I'd get in big trouble if that happened."

Elizabeth turned to Paul.

"Henry Baumsdorfer would blame me. And probably he'd send me home and that would be that for our family's Cairo experience."

Paul jumped into the conversation.

"As a man who speaks in plain English, Maggie, I have to say that it sure seems like something's bugging you."

"No, not really."

Maggie finished her breakfast. If she really was the one person meant to save Bubastis as Oum believed, then she had to begin taking some chances. She had to get involved.

Maggie stared at a point on the table. Her parents exchanged a look. They were taken completely off guard when Maggie jumped up from the table and announced:

"There's something I have to show you. Wait here."

Maggie went out the front door and down the hall. She peered into the carton. The mother cat greeted her with a sleepy meow. Maggie regarded the cat family. Taking care of them made her feel so good. Just seeing her tee shirt under the kittens—suddenly Maggie was struck with a thought. That cotton tee shirt. The old peach one she had dug out of the laundry. Maggie wondered where the cotton it was made of had come from. The shirt was something she had bought early last summer at some shop, Lily's Closet or some other place, without a second thought. But its fibers had to come from somewhere. Could it be Egyptian cotton? And if so, where had that cotton been woven into fabric? And where had the fabric been sewn into a shirt that some random American girl could buy? And who did all this work? Suddenly Maggie became aware of not knowing where things really came from. Everyday things. Things that people just had. It was dizzying. The mother cat opened her mouth.

"*MAU.*"

"Sorry. Just got a little distracted there. I think I've got cotton on the brain. Anyway, I bet you're tired after the day you had yesterday. But you can go ahead and tell your friends that I got the message. Now, if you'll excuse me, it's time for me to take one of these little guys. And I'm sure you know who. After all, I am the throne of the white cat, remember? Oum said."

She bent down and gently lifted up the white kitten along with the peach-colored tee shirt. In her arms the kitten chirped faintly. Maggie raised the warm ball of fur to her cheek. It was so warm, so filled with life. It purred against her face. Maggie felt a surge of energy and hope. The only thing that worried her was her mom, or at least her mom's work. Somehow helping the cats would mean getting in Elizabeth's way. Maggie knew this, and glanced at the mother cat.

"What can I do but what I have to do?"

The mother cat closed her eyes. The two other kittens remained sleeping.

"It's you, my sweet pet," Maggie murmured to the white kitten. "You and I have to get to work around here. Let's go." Maggie turned back to the mother cat.

"Thank you."

"*MAU*," the cat replied. Maggie bowed her head.

She returned to the apartment with the white kitten tucked under her chin.

"Check it out."

"Maggie!"

"They were born down the hall in an old Nike carton. I've been feeding them a little bit every day. They know me. Mom, Dad, I think you guys know what I'm going to ask."

Maggie was glad she had waited a few days before making her request. The words seemed to flow effortlessly from her lips. She was not stuttering at all. Just then it occurred to her that since the encounter in Room 54, she hadn't stammered once.

Her parents seemed stunned. Naturally they were surprised to hear that their daughter had been feeding a stray cat, but they seemed even more surprised to hear Maggie continue to speak without a hitch. In the past, her spells of fluency were always broken by some impossible consonant. As she made her case for keeping the kitten, her parents seemed to sense a connection between her excitement over the kitten and her new fluency. Luckily for Maggie, Paul was ready to label just about anything in Cairo a magical learning experience. You could learn a lot, he assured his wife, from keeping a little kitten in a foreign country for a year.

"I guess we don't have to decide right now what to do with this cat when it's time to go home," Elizabeth said.

"Of course not," Maggie said. "We have loads of time."

Maggie gave her parents a hug and went off carrying the kitten. She had to find something to use as a litter box. She laid the small creature down on her bed and inspected it from head to toe.

"Now you need a name."

The kitten looked up with round green eyes. The pads on the bottom of her paws were pink. Briskly licking, she began to clean each leg in turn.

Maggie knew the Arabic name for cat was *quttah*. That sounded like Kitty, but was too general. And also, she wanted a name that reached farther back in time than Arabic did. She wanted something from Bastet's time, from old Egypt time. And she wanted a name that would identify this cat as a singular being in the service of MAU. Sarah belonged to Maggie. This cat would belong to MAU. What should MAU's familiar be called?

Maggie thought about the first time she heard herself called by the name of MAU. It had been when she was standing beneath the obelisk at Heliopolis on Thursday, only three days ago. That was it! Maybe hieroglyphs would give her an idea. The word she sought was Kitten. But the ancient Egyptians used no vowels. Kitten without vowels would be K-T-N. Maggie ran into the living room and got the guidebook. She opened to the page explaining hieroglyphics and spoke aloud to the white kitten, who was now sound asleep in a tight little ball.

"K, K...the K sound is a basket. T is a loaf, like a loaf of bread. And N...hm...N is that zigzag worm shape again. Maybe I ought to write it down and see what we've got here."

She pulled her composition book from under her pillow. She turned to a fresh page. On the paper, in a single row, she drew the hieroglyphic symbols that spelled KTN:

"Hm."

The first image, the basket, reminded Maggie of the Moses story, especially since the third image, the zigzag shape that meant N, represented water, which could be the water of the Nile. But what, Maggie wondered, did any of that have to do with this little white kitten? Maggie *had* drawn the kitten out of a basket, of sorts. But what about the loaf? K-T-N: a basket, a loaf, and water. Maybe she was on the wrong track entirely. Maybe some things just couldn't or shouldn't be translated. Maggie sat for a moment before bounding into the living room and firing up the laptop. She clicked on Google, then typed the words *Egyptian Girl Names*. She clicked on a web site and began to scroll down. It wasn't long before her eyes lit up. There it was: *Aziza*. It meant precious treasure. Of course! This little white kitten was her very own Egyptian treasure. Forward or backward its meaning was the same. From the first letter of the alphabet to the last. Aziza was another magical word—like Zagazig. In fact, letter for letter, Aziza had been hiding in Zagazig all along. Maggie dashed back into her room.

"I name you Aziza," she said to the tiny ball of white curled up on her bed.

Aziza gave a tiny mew.

The Bastet figurine lay under her pillow. Maggie retrieved it and kissed its cool forehead. She stood it up on the desk and sat back down in her chair. Then she spoke to it very quietly.

"Thank you for making my stutter go away. Now I know for sure you want me to speak. But what do you want me to say?"

Chapter 14
Bubasteion

Maggie closed the composition book. The white square on the cover said *All the Cats of Cairo*. On the second line, she now wrote "*MAU*" in hieroglyphs—the owl, the eagle, and the quail—just like the markings on the obelisk in Heliopolis.

There, she thought. I can always separate the private parts from the public parts some other time. Right now I can't be bothered with knowing which is which. She tucked the book back under her pillow.

By now her parents were dressed. The tall lanky form of her father appeared in her doorway fresh from a shower.

"So what's on the agenda today, Maggie? I have a plan to visit the world's oldest stone monument."

"You mean the Great Pyramid? I thought you said that would be too crowded on a weekend."

Paul registered Maggie's newly confident voice and raised his index finger up in the air.

"Ah, but the pyramids at Giza are not the oldest. We're going a little ways up the Nile to Saqqara to see the famous step pyramid of Zoser. The Great Pyramid is the biggest. But I'd like to see the oldest."

Maggie threw up her hands. "Dad, everything we visit here is either the oldest or the largest or the biggest."

"Very true."

"Egypt is extremely extreme."

"Well, I'm afraid Saqqara will be another extreme destination. Most of the Old Kingdom pharoahs are buried there. Along with their wives and servants, I might add, who tended to be sacrificed and buried with their ruler."

'That's awful," Maggie said.

"That's the way it was. Wives and children were buried alive."

"What a terrible thing. I don't think I want to be in a place where that kind of stuff happened."

Maggie thought about it a little more. Even if the proposed trip had been some place more appealing, she just didn't want to stick with her parents today. There was too much to do. She had to get in touch with Tareq and find out what he learned yesterday before the party at the museum. She was sure he must have heard something worth knowing. She also needed to find out who Ramsey had been dealing with when she overheard him at the museum. She wished there was some way of getting in touch with Tareq that didn't require walking all the way back to the Northern Cemetery. With any luck maybe he'd be lurking about in her neighborhood again, or keeping Oum company at her poultry stall on the market street nearby. It seemed as if the only way she could get any answers would be on her own, away from her parents. Certainly it was the only way she could do the work of *MAU*. Maybe she could convince them to leave her behind for the day.

Paul remained in the doorway leafing through his guide book.

"I think this complex was also a necropolis for sacred animals," he said as he thumbed through pages. "Apart from the burial chambers for bulls, cows, ibises, hawks, baboons, and dogs, there's this place called the Bubastieion tombs, where some cat goddess was worshipped."

On the other hand, Maggie thought, maybe I'll pick some other time to hang back.

A wheezing taxi carried Maggie and her parents west across the Nile on Al-Haram, also known as Pyramids Road. Maggie looked out the window at the angled white sails of the feluccas. Stretched belly-full of wind, they cruised speedily upstream. The slower river buses left small white caps of waves in their wake. It felt good to leave the cramped, smoggy, sprawling center of downtown Cairo. She was glad she'd come along, even though it meant a delay in catching up with Tareq and leaving Aziza shut up in the bathroom all day with food, water and a litter box.

Maggie was also excited to explore a place devoted to Bastet. Maybe she'd be able to learn a thing or two before the time came to visit Bubastis up north. Maggie stroked the figurine in her pocket.

Heavy Sunday traffic clogged the fifteen-mile route to Saqqara. Snarled among tour buses, minivans, and other cars, their taxi was either lurching forward or coming to a dead stop. Finally, after almost an hour, they swung around to the western side of the great Giza plateau. As their driver gestured excitedly toward the landscape of pyramids, Maggie tried to take in the scale of the huge structures. She couldn't believe how puny the swarms of people looked from this perspective. Of course she knew the cliché but this time it was true: the circulating population of tourists, guides, guards, vendors, and beasts of burden really did seem like ants crawling around the base of a playground climber. The taxi continued south past the pyramids toward their destination.

A few minutes later the taxi dropped them off, already broiling hot, at North Saqqara. Maggie was relieved to find a much smaller crowd here than at Giza and she looked around. Right behind them was a site called the Serapeum. Maggie swigged from one of her three water bottles and consulted the guidebook.

"This place is a burial spot for the sacred Apis bulls," she read aloud, thinking that if sacred bulls were buried there, maybe sacred cats wouldn't be too far way. "I think we ought to go in there—wait a minute! Look!"

She directed her parents' attention to a clump of pack animals tethered nearby. There were camels, donkeys, and a few lean horses. Their owners stood in a huddle beside them.

"Please?"

"Please what, Maggie?"

"Please can we hire camels to explore this place?"

Her father consented. Maggie was ecstatic.

Dozens of dusty gray camels lay in the sand with their front legs folded beneath them. Single strands of rope were knotted to their halters, and colorful woven blankets covered their backs in patterned shades of red, black, and white. Wooden pegs stuck up from their saddles.

Paul negotiated with a cheerful camel driver for three animals, one for each of them. A trip around the area would cost thirty Egyptian pounds total. The driver placed a stool on the ground beside the first camel and invited Maggie to mount.

Approaching, she looked into the deep glassy black eye of the camel. Its lashes were long and thick. The animal steadily ground its cud. Wiry whiskers on the camel's cleft top lip twitched at tiny desert flies. Maggie threw a long leg over the saddle and balanced herself on the camel's warm back. She felt a powerful rocking motion as the animal shifted its weight from front to back and stabilized onto its knees. She gripped the wooden peg tightly. Gusts of wind blew sand into her hair and eyes. She kept her lips closed so the swirling sand wouldn't get inside her mouth. She hated the feeling of sand crunching in her molars. Another heave and the camel was up and moving on its feet. There was nothing to do but hold on and look around.

What she saw were tombs, tombs, and more tombs. Dead pharoahs. Dead wives. Dead servants. Dead children. Dead animals. Not even a green plant sprouting anywhere in sight, only sand and stone and bones. As Maggie rocked back and forth on what everyone called her ship of the desert, her lips pressed closed against the sand, Maggie found herself constantly confronted with the idea of death. Huge stone structures, small mounds, rocks and bricks and carved stone—all built for the dead.

Off her camel and exploring the tomb interiors, Maggie saw detailed paintings of daily life. There were also shelves of small household objects like makeup jars and combs, and statuettes and figurines, all things once handled by the ancient Egyptians. Real people of those days had built, painted, crafted, and assembled a whole virtual city for people and animals who no longer lived in their actual bodies, but were expected to live in the next world just as they had in this one. Just like the Northern Cemetery where Tareq lived, this place was layered with life—donkeys, horses, camels, tourists from all over the world, taxi drivers, bus drivers, animal renters.

Maggie was struck by the drawings decorating the surfaces of the sarcophagi, walls, and statues. Lions, hedgehogs, cows, and chickens, each one painted in detail. In other paintings she saw images of young boys playing. Some of the captions—according to her guide—were actually jokes. Ancient Egypt's version of *Zits*. On one wall Maggie saw a picture of a man visiting a doctor. She asked the guide about it and he said that the caption said something like "Hold him steady now, so he doesn't fall and get hurt." The joke didn't strike Maggie as particularly hilarious.

"I guess it was funny to whoever wrote it," she said.

Still, Maggie thought, as she returned to her camel after walking the dark passages on foot, these tombs celebrate life, real daily life. Maybe this is what people mean when they talk about eternal life. Remembering stuff.

All afternoon the hot sun lit up everything around her, and Maggie found herself thinking about the terms that had seemed so foreign and confusing. If *ka* is the eternal vital force animating all of creation, and *ba* is the spirit of individual selves, then *ka* somehow contains both the *ba* of the dead and the *ba* of the living. Maybe Bastet is really all about *ka*, Maggie thought. The vital energy connecting everything that ever was with everything there is now. Maybe our *ka* is all out of whack, and that's why she needs help, to restore balance to the energy of the universe. Maybe Ramsey's project is the final straw, which is why Bastet needs all of us little *bas* to help fix things.

Maggie looked with new eyes at the tombs. Even if their bodies are dead, Maggie thought, the ancient Egyptians have achieved eternal life, in a way. Because their spirits—their *bas*—are bumping up against our *bas* in a great pool of *ka*. By envisioning their actual existence, which we do when we read about them on these tomb walls, we are bringing them to life in our imagination. And they are adding their spirits to the life we are living here and now. Because now we know about them, and before coming here we did not. Their past lives are a part of our present life. Therefore everyone who has ever lived creates a shared future. Every *ba* that ever was and ever will be can help fix the messed up *ka*.

In an instant, Maggie had a sense of all of creation's vital energy surrounding her like an infinitely huge ocean of *ka*—a unity of all being. She was just a tiny bit of *ba* adrift in this sea of spirit. It was thrilling, but also terrifying. Thousands of years collapsed into single moment. Billions of people converged into a single soul. She felt dizzy.

"Maggie!"

Elizabeth's panicked voiced called her out of the trance-like state.

"Maggie, are you okay? It looked like you were about to fall off."

For the rest of the afternoon Maggie and her parents passed back and forth between the bright hot light of the desert into the cold darkness of the tombs. Close to four o'clock, Elizabeth said she needed a break. Paul offered to keep his wife company if Maggie wanted to explore one more tomb on her own. She did. It was the moment she'd been waiting for.

"I think I'll just mosey over by foot to that tomb called Bubastieion," she said. "I'll meet you back here."

After hours of rocking along on the back of a camel, it felt good to be walking on solid, if sandy, ground. It also felt good to be relatively alone. Maggie trekked purposefully to the eastern side of the site. The last of the giant tour buses had pulled away for the day, and guards were beginning to lock up the monuments.

Maggie arrived at the ancient cat burial ground. She didn't have her hopes up about finding anything more than ruins. What she had experienced all day long made her realize that just being at the site was the important thing. To put her *ba*—the *ba* of *MAU*—where people once worshiped Bastet.

Bubastieion was a disappointment, no more than a square marked off in the rocky sand. Archaeologists had obviously been working on the site for some time. Yellow rope cordoned off several portions of the place. Printed signs indicated ongoing explorations and reminders. At first Maggie couldn't even really tell where the temple had stood and where the graves were arranged. Scattered around the lot were several large carved pillars, a few tiny sarcophagi, and rubble. Lots of rubble. Maggie turned when she heard a guard shout. She figured he wanted to close the place up and get the tourists out.

"One moment, please," she called back to him.

Maggie walked around a broken column and sat down. It was still blazing hot, but at least her head was in the shade. She closed her eyes and tried to absorb whatever energy might come her way. Maggie didn't know exactly what she was expecting—a vision or an image; a message or a sign—but she certainly wasn't expecting to hear a perfectly normal and real-world snuffling sound.

Maggie got up and moved in the direction of the sound. About twenty feet away, on the other side of another broken pillar, a young child sat curled up in a ball hugging his knees. He wore a torn and dirty long white shirt. The toenails of his bare feet were jagged and black with dirt, his shaggy black hair matted with sand and mud. And he was trying to stifle sobs.

Maggie plumbed her brain for the smattering of conversational Arabic she knew. She prayed that her stutter would not return just at this moment.

"*Salam 'alekum,*" she said. "Hi. Do you speak any English? *Enta bititkallim inglizi?*"

The boy didn't reply.

"My Arabic is non-existent, really. I wonder if you're lost. Where is your mommy? *Fein mama?*"

Curiosity won out over misery; the boy peeked out over his folded arms to see who was trying to communicate with him. Maggie spoke again.

"*Ismi Maggie. Ismak eh?*"

"*Ismi Hassan.*"

"Hi, Hassan."

Maggie extended her hand to the unhappy boy. He reached out, tweaked her fingers, and gave a limp shake. She guessed he was about six years old.

"I can see that you are sad, but I have no idea why." Maggie squatted down in front of him. "I bet I look totally strange to you."

It was obvious that the sound of her prattling was calming him. The boy's eyes widened in wonder at this large pale person. Maggie removed her backpack and reached in for one of the unopened bottles of water. She unscrewed the top and held the bottle out to the boy. He wiped his sleeve along the running wetness under his nose.

Maggie extended her arm further toward his hand and nodded.

"It's okay. It's only water. Water? See?"

The boy took the bottle and gulped water. Some went down his windpipe and he coughed. Then he drank some more. He was mostly skin and bones. Maggie guessed he couldn't have weighed more than forty pounds.

A sharp voice approached, apparently scolding the child. It was the guard who had been calling to Maggie. Clearly, he hadn't known the child was there. The boy had been hiding. But why? And why in Bubastieion?

The guard grabbed the boy by the shoulder and yanked him to his feet. He spoke more angry words, then turned to Maggie and apologized.

"Sorry, Miss. Boy no belong here. Very sorry."

Maggie was unfazed.

"It's no big deal. I was just hanging out. And I heard him crying. He seems upset about something."

The boy scratched the guard's face and broke away. He spoke directly to Maggie in a torrent of feeling. Sure that he was revealing the reason for his sadness, she was furious with herself for not being able to understand.

"What does he say?" she asked the guard.

The guard waved away the boy's despair and dabbed at his face with a cloth. The boy's jagged nails had broken skin. "My nephew. He sad because family want to keep him living. Come now. Saqqara closing. If you want to stay I can arrange for small fee, for *baksheesh*." He held out his hand and rubbed his thumb against the tips of his four other fingers.

Maggie was completely confused.

"Wait a minute. I don't want you to keep this place open for me. I want to know what you mean. Why would he be sad if his family is trying to save his life?"

The boy jabbered incomprehensibly to Maggie. The guard sighed.

"Family very poor. Not enough food. Boy can go work in north. Shelter and food for him, money for family. He not want to leave home."

Maggie tried to assemble the pieces of this broken story. It seemed to her that the guard was trying to say that the boy's family was poor. In exchange for a fee, his family found a way to send the boy into some kind of service in the north. He would be fed, clothed, and housed, and the family would receive money.

"I can understand he might not like this," she said. "But why does he seem so hysterical? Is his mother going along with this? I think there's something more he's trying to tell me."

It was closing time, and Maggie could tell that the guard was fed up. No doubt he had spent another day tolerating the presence of rich tourists. His face was bleeding. His nephew was becoming an embarrassment before an American. He had nothing more to hide.

"Because other boys go from village and not come back. His big brother never come back again. That is why. Our boys go and not return."

Maggie was aghast. She spelled out each word slowly and distinctly.

"It sounds like you are saying that these kids are not being hired, they are being bought."

The guard shrugged. "Hired. Bought. These are your words. Here in Egypt, work is work. They stay away to work. It is no bad thing."

A second guard, mounted on a dusty donkey, trotted over. While the boy looked up at her with pleading eyes full of tears, the two guards gesticulated excitedly and spoke together. The donkey stamped the ground with his hind hoofs. Maggie watched the faces of the men. They were trying to make a decision. The boy's uncle wanted one thing, the second guard another. She looked from the men to the boy, and back to the men. It seemed that they were trying to decide his fate. Finally the uncle made a proposition that made her blood run cold.

"You pay more good money for boy? He safe with you. Help with the parents and the work. Will live in America?"

"I cannot buy this little boy," Maggie replied, doing her best to keep calm. She couldn't believe she was spelling out why she couldn't buy a child. "He is a human being who lives with his family."

The guard snorted. "With his family he starves. With you he lives. You have Egyptian pounds, no? In bag?"

Narrowing his eyes, he indicated Maggie's backpack. He placed his hand on Maggie's forearm. The second guard turned away in disgust.

Maggie was afraid. What could she do? If she turned and ran back to her parents, she'd be abandoning the little child who was crying again softly. If she stayed, she would be putting herself in a dangerous position.

And then a great heat began to surge up from the ground through her shoes and into the soles of her feet. The warmth spread up through each leg, circling around her knees, and flowing into her hips and stomach. Heat spread inside the cage of her ribs and through her heart. It was almost as if an earthly force had raised the temperature of her blood from

98.6 to 120 degrees. Her arms grew hot, then her neck, and finally the hot blood sensation began to course around her brain and behind her eyes. She felt as though she were growing larger, swelling out from the internal pressure of the heat. It was like what happened in the museum the night before, but about a thousand times more intense. The guard flinched and pulled his hand off Maggie's arm. Evidently he, too, sensed the heat suffusing her flesh. He stared at her wide-eyed with fear.

From somewhere deep in the sand beneath her feet, a low rumbling sound made the ground tremble. All around, a haze of sand rose up from the desert floor and blurred the line between earth and sky. The donkey laid its ears back and brayed. The second guard tried to calm the animal, but it reared away from the touch of the hand and pulled back against the tight hemp rope attached to the bridle. The guards looked at each other.

"Haza ardeyah!" the boy's uncle cried. *"Earthquake!"*

The rumbling of the earth continued. As if materializing out of the very rock and stone that formed Bubastieion, thirty cats appeared. It was no longer safe for them to remain inside the underground chambers of the tomb and temple. Tails up, hair on end, ears laid back, lips curled in displeasure, they meowed shrilly. From all sides they approached Maggie. This was the sign Maggie had been waiting for. As the quake subsided she scooped up the little boy and held him on her hip. She watched him carefully, but he did not seem to be burned by her touch. Maggie looked at the circling cats and spoke to the guards with confidence.

"I know where to find you. I will take the boy with me for now and clean him and feed him. I will bring him back here tomorrow. He trusts me. Explain to him what I'm doing. Then explain to his mother in the village that he will come back. Tomorrow."

The guard was quick in reply. Even if this American were sent from Allah, he needed collateral. He kicked a brown cat away from his ankle.

"I need security for his possession."

"Security?"

"You leave me something. I give back when boy comes back. Tomorrow, as you say." He kicked a second cat. Regaining its balance, this cat joined the others grouped behind Maggie.

Maggie thought about what she had in her backpack. A half a bottle of water. The Bastet figurine. No way would she part with that. And she knew better than to even consider letting her passport get out of sight. She did have the earrings she was wearing. They were her favorite dangly stars, the going away gift from James. Silver five-pointed stars inlaid with turquoise. Although the chances were good she'd never see the earrings again, Maggie pulled them out one by one and handed them to the guard. He examined them closely.

"No dollars?"

It made her sick to her stomach to take away a child for a mere twenty dollars, but she gave the guard the bills and walked away with Hassan. Although she knew he didn't understand a word, she went on speaking soothingly.

"You don't know what in the world is going on, but anything is better than what that creepy uncle of yours has got planned. Somehow, we are going to figure out what's up around here, and where your brother and all the other boys have gone. I have an idea, of course, but it's too early to say anything to anybody."

As Maggie walked back toward the step pyramid, surrounded by the pack of cats and holding Hassan on her hip, the boy examined the hole in her earlobe. There had been a shiny star there a few moments ago, but now it was gone.

"Hassan, James will never believe what happened to those earrings. And it is quite likely that my parents will have a conniption when they realize we're taking you home for the night. So just stay calm, okay? I won't panic if you don't panic."

Hugging her tighter, Hassan clung like a koala. Maggie addressed the cats.

"You take off now. I'll be lucky if I can explain Hassan here. I definitely cannot explain you."

Chapter 15

Resources on the Line

"What the hell was that?" Ramsey blurted, watching his iced tea shiver in its glass and feeling the hotel terrace vibrate. He was wearing a yellow polo jersey and lime green golf trousers. His pink feet and horny yellow toenails were bare. His shock of thick white hair had not been pomaded into place. To tell the truth, he was not feeling what he might have called "one hundred percent jack rabbit ready." After the cocktail party, Baumsdorfer from the embassy had taken him and the young French secretary out to a few clubs. Ramsey had barely moved all day. Now Nazaret and Tareq were standing side by side in Ramsey's suite, just inside the open sliding glass door to the terrace.

Ramsey was sitting with Minister Mahfouz. The heat of the day had passed, and in the slanting rays of the sun the wide and mighty Nile sparkled in deep shades of blue and green as it flowed steadily north. Like an anchored ship, the island of Gezira split the river. And from the prow of the ship, the Gezira Sheraton provided an ideal spot from which to enjoy this lovely Sunday evening. The noisy rhythmic din of Cairo was across the channel to the east. Dusty date palms lining the shore swayed in the evening breeze. Sunset prayers were minutes away.

"Sometimes we have these, Mr. Ramsey. They are nothing at all to worry about."

"Well, I'll be damned. An earthquake."

"Our seismologists say that as long as they are small they are good. The small ones relieve some of the pressure so that we might avoid experiencing a large one as we did in 1992. Do you mind if I smoke?"

"Go right ahead. Please. As a matter of fact, I just might light up one of these here cigars I had brought up from Cuba last spring when a friend of mine was down there buyin' up art. Can I interest you in a Cohiba, Mr. Mahfouz?" He offered the cigar with his left hand. The minister winced slightly.

"Thank you, no." Exhaling a stream of blue smoke, the minister tried not to look down at Ramsey's calloused and peeling feet. The American seemed utterly unaware of the fact that showing the soles of one's feet to an Egyptian was considered grossly insulting. Sometimes, the minister mused bitterly, doing his job meant looking the other way. Four stories above the leafy oasis of Gezira, Minister Mahfouz was doing his job. He glanced into the suite, where Nazaret and Tareq stood.

"You know, Mr. Mahfouz, I am expecting to leave Egypt on Wednesday with our arrangements all sewn up."

"I certainly hope that nothing will frustrate your intentions, Mr. Ramsey."

"I don't expect anything will. But I confess I would like to see a little more action over there in Zagazig before I go back home."

"Action, sir?"

Ramsey chuckled and took a noisy sip of his iced tea.

"I don't mind tellin' you, sir, that some of my family members are lookin' upon this investment with what we call a gimlet eye. We Ramseys go way back in this here cotton endeavor, and I cannot go home with merely a signed piece of paper. I need to be able to tell them that I have seen with my own eyes the ole John Deeres startin' to get down and dirty at the site. I need to assure them with some digital camera proof that y'all are going to be able to do what you say you are going to do."

"I see."

"Now accordin' to my itinerary, we have a walk-through tomorrow and then some sort of a grand tour and groundbreaking set up for Tuesday."

"Yes, Mr. Ramsey."

"You, me, Moussa, and our little Lizzie McKee over at the embassy are scheduled to drive up there and check things out."

"Yes, Mr. Ramsey."

The minister leaned forward and mashed out his cigarette more vigorously than he customarily did.

"I'd like you, Mr. Mahfouz, to make doubly sure that you do whatever is humanly possible to get together the evidence I need. Do you understand me, Mr. Mahfouz?"

"I believe I do, Mr. Ramsey."

"Let me make myself even clearer, Mr. Mahfouz," Ramsey went on, blind to the look of displeasure on the face of the Egyptian. "I will not be able to transfer the funds we have negotiated unless and until I see that you people are as committed to putting your own resources on the line as I am."

The trade minister weighed his words carefully.

"You have made yourself extremely clear, Mr. Ramsey. I believe I can guarantee that all of the collaborating parties will be pleased on Tuesday."

Ramsey sat back in his wrought iron terrace chair and crossed his ankle over his knee. He stirred his iced tea and took another sip.

"Glad to hear it, sir. I am very glad to hear it."

Inside the suite, Tareq was beginning to understand that it wasn't only poor people who had to swallow pride.

A few blocks north of the Sheraton, an uncomfortably quiet foursome was zipping by taxi across the Galaa bridge onto the island of Gezira. Maggie and her mother sat on either side of Hassan in the back seat. Paul was sitting with the driver in front. Maggie knew that her parents were upset and angry. This wasn't like buying a locally crafted wooden hair clasp. This wasn't even like adopting a stray kitten. She had taken responsibility for a human being. Even her parents, who generally encouraged her to get involved in extracurricular activities, seemed shocked. Partly they were exhausted from the day's exploration in the blazing heat. And partly, of course, they were struck dumb by the minor earthquake. When Maggie approached them carrying Hassan, they were so relieved to see her safe that her request didn't seem as unthinkable as it might have if she'd come home from school in D.C. with a strange child on her hip.

Maggie considered the strangeness of the situation. If it didn't feel so intense right now she might have tried to get her parents to laugh, or at least say something. But how could she even begin to humor them? There wasn't anything funny about what she was doing.

Hassan remained still as a mouse leaning against Maggie. She put her arm around his shoulders and could tell that he trusted her. Feeling his warm weight, she was sure that she had done the right thing. And she was also sure that with Tareq's help she would be able to figure out what was going on with the village boys. She was sure that it had something to do with the cats of Bubastis but she couldn't be sure how. Or why. And she only had a day. A single day to figure out what was going on and get Hassan back to his own family. She'd told Hassan's uncle she'd be back by Monday's evening prayers.

"I think we ought to agree that this...this..." Elizabeth was at a loss for words. She started again. "I think we need to understand that what Maggie has done, is doing, doesn't leave this family."

Paul turned to the backseat. "I agree. Obviously, Maggie made an emergency decision. But this is not something any of us can talk about with anyone. Maggie? Are we clear on that?"

"Very clear."

"We are trusting you, Maggie," Elizabeth said, putting her hand a little too firmly on Maggie shoulder. "I will lose my job if anyone finds out about this. You have put me in a very difficult position."

Maggie exploded. "How can you say that? How can you say that you're in a difficult position when Hassan was just offered for sale, when his brother has been basically sold off. How can any position you could possibly be in be worse than that?"

The look she received from her mother chilled the heat of her rage. Maggie felt Hassan tremble and stopped herself from speaking more.

Elizabeth spoke quietly. "You don't know what has happened to Hassan's brother, Maggie. All you have is the translated word of a very little boy. This whole thing is craziness. If it hadn't been for the earthquake, I doubt very much we'd be having this conversation."

Maggie looked out the window. How could she tell her parents about the heat that roared up in her body whenever the spirit of Bastet came to her? She couldn't. And yet it was that power that made her sure she was not engaged in what her mother called pure craziness. The heat was real. The power was real. She was even beginning to wonder if she herself—armed with Bastet's power—had caused the earthquake.

The taxi came to the east side of the Qasr el-Nil Bridge and plunged into downtown Cairo. No one said a word the rest of the way home.

Shut up in the bathroom, Aziza had weathered the day perfectly well. The white kitten had used the litter box and drunk all the water. She'd also torn up a few brochures lying around on the floor. Hassan was instantly enamored of the kitten, who scampered about ready to play. It was the first time Maggie saw Hassan smile; his baby teeth were like little white shells. Maggie let him play while she found a clean towel, a tee shirt, and a pair of her smallest boxers. She drew a warm bath and found a few items from the kitchen—a sponge, a plastic cup, a strainer—that even a six year old might want to play with in the water. Then she carried Hassan piggy-back into the bathroom.

The boy was young enough not to feel embarrassed by Maggie's care. When she saw him naked, Maggie could not believe how skinny and dirty he was.

"I wouldn't have thought a person could be so caked in mud and grime. We're going to need the loofah to get you clean."

Hassan sat down in the tub. He submerged the sponge and watched it pop up full of water while Maggie got to work. Washing his hair was the hardest part. Maggie had to shampoo twice and use conditioner to get out all the matted tangles. With her growing fingernails she scratched out the mud that caked his hair in sections. When she was finally finished, she drained the dirty water and refilled the tub with clean. Then she let Aziza into the bathroom to watch Hassan play. The kitten leaped onto the rim of the tub and balanced there. The light-catching movement of the water transfixed the kitten's gaze. Watching her, Hassan giggled. Maggie sat on the floor beside the tub and watched them both. She was dying to find Tareq and get a real translation of what Hassan had to say. She was also sure that after a second day of his so-called driving training, Tareq would have a great deal to tell her about what he was learning. But all of it would have to wait until morning.

Maggie got Hassan out of the tub, dried and dressed him, ran a comb through his hair, and presented him fresh and clean at the dinner table.

Hassan ate greedily with his fingers. He loved everything Maggie put on his plate. Chicken. Noodles with butter and salt. Boiled spinach. Pita. Even the mixed salad of mangos, oranges, bananas, and papaya. He drank three glasses of milk.

"Mom, I was thinking that I could make a sort of nest for Hassan on the floor of my room. It's just one night, and I could take the cushions from the sofa and cover them with an extra sheet. Would that be okay?"

"That would be fine."

"What exactly is your plan, Maggie?" Paul asked. Maggie could tell that both her parents were still mad.

"We're going to go over to Tareq's. He and Oum can help me understand what Hassan was trying to tell me this afternoon. I didn't trust that uncle one bit. I know you said we can't talk about this with anyone, but they can be trusted. And they'll help me get him home again later. I promise."

Elizabeth looked like she was going to protest. But then, to Maggie's surprise, nothing more was said.

Unaccustomed to eating such a large meal at one sitting, Hassan grew sleepy. He yawned again and again. By way of signaling that it was time for bed, Maggie made her hands into a prayer position and pressed them against her cheek. Then she tipped her head and hands to her shoulder as if lying down.

"Time for night-night Hassan."

The boy got off his chair, crawled onto Maggie's lap, and threw his arms around her neck. Maggie carried him into her bedroom. She laid him on her own bed and Aziza jumped up beside him. The kitten and the boy watched Maggie with sleepy eyes; by the time the makeshift bed was arranged, Hassan was sound asleep. Maggie transferred his sleeping form down onto the bed of cushions and tucked him in. Aziza hopped down to be next to him. Maggie got the Bastet figurine from her backpack and slipped it under his pillow.

"Good night, Hassan," she whispered. "Lie down now, little Aziza. That's it. Good night, Bastet. Guard him well."

Maggie helped with the dinner clean-up. Drying the dishes in silence, she sensed the hard feelings. Still, she was sure she was doing the right thing, even if her parents were not. She said good night and went to her room.

Hassan was on his back snoring faintly. Aziza was curled at his temple, her white coat contrasting with his long black hair. Maggie looked at these two little beings. There lay her duty, in black and white. She would do right by them.

In the peace and quiet of her room Maggie sat down at her desk with her composition book and wrote for a few minutes.

Before getting into her own bed she kneeled down by Hassan's side and prayed silently. It wasn't the kind of prayer she'd ever heard or uttered before.

Dear Bastet, I believe that there is more than the destruction of your sacred temple at stake. I believe that there are dark forces threatening your people in the delta of the Nile. Please, Bastet, continue to let me serve your interest. I want to help restore the ka. *I will always try to honor your call. And I will take good care of all who help me to serve you. Amen.*

Maggie got into bed and lay down on her back. She stared at the cracks in the ceiling and listened to the sound of Hassan breathing before falling asleep.

Chapter 16

Missing Persons

SOON AFTER THE SUNRISE PRAYERS, even before her parents were awake, Maggie and Hassan were on their way to the Northern Cemetery. She'd left her parents a note explaining that she was getting an early start. She also wrote that she'd be back before nightfall. She filled Aziza's bowl with fresh water and put a little bit of leftover chicken on a plastic yogurt lid.

As soon as they were outside, Hassan motioned that he was hungry. Maggie stopped at a vendor and bought him an order of *fuul* and a glass of fresh orange juice. Not far from the apartment they met Tareq.

"Maggie!" Tareq said. *"Sabah al-kher!* Good morning! To you I was coming this day. Very early now. I have much to tell."

"Hi, Tareq! I am so glad to bump into you." Maggie let go of Hassan's small hand and shook her friend's cordially.

"Bump me?"

"Not bump you. Bump into you. Another expression for your collection. It means, 'have an unintentional encounter.'"

Maggie could tell by Tareq's face that the long words were a mistake. He still didn't get it. She waved it away.

"Oh, never mind. Listen Tareq, this is Hassan. Hassan, Tareq."

Tareq looked down at the little boy in the strangely fitting American clothes and bare feet. He patted Hassan on the head.

"*Fursa sa 'ida.*"

"*Ahlan we sahlan.*"

And then the boys were talking a mile a minute. Maggie didn't have a clue what they were saying. She could tell when Hassan began to explain how he met Maggie, because his face got extremely animated as he acted out the rough voice of his uncle. He also made a booming sound and waved his hands in the air, which was probably a rendition of the earthquake. Here Maggie jumped in to the conversation. Even though she was excited, she tried to speak slowly and in simple phrases.

"Tareq, we need to speak to Oum. We need to find out what is happening to the brother of Hassan. We need to find out where these boys are going. And also, I need to know what you've heard while driving around with Nazaret. Will you come with me back to his boat?"

Tareq seemed to be following her pretty accurately. "Nazaret will be car driver almost all day. Felucca driver later."

"Maybe he could give us a ride up the river to Saqqara when it is time for Hassan to go home."

"Perhaps."

"Tareq, do you want to go to Oum with me and speak about these things?"

"Oum already selling birds. She go to Al-Muizz li-Din market street to sell. I take you there now."

Oddly, given that Tareq was a perfect stranger to Hassan, the young boy took the older boy's hand. He bounced along between the two older children, swinging Maggie's hand on his right and Tareq's on his left. A peculiar feeling came over Maggie. She felt so protective of Hassan, and also so pleased that Tareq should be walking along too. It felt right that he should be with them. They were sort of like a little family. She looked over Hassan's head at Tareq. He caught her eye and looked away shyly. Did he have that peculiar feeling too?

"I think minister is not happy with Ramsey," Tareq said, getting right to the point as usual.

"Do you know why?" Maggie asked.

"He is not happy with the man. But I think he is also unhappy with the project." Tareq paused, evidently struggling over how to express what he had half sensed, half understood. "Maybe not unhappy. More like feeling two feelings. Torn inside."

"Hm."

"I also think I understood that something is going to happen tomorrow at Zagazig," Tareq said. "Some ceremony. I do not understand. Ramsey wants to see smoke, but this again I do not understand. He wants John Deere to be working and smoking. Who is John Deere?"

Maggie was concentrating so hard, but at this innocent question she turned such an affectionate face to Tareq the boy was puzzled.

"John Deere is not a person," Maggie said. "John Deere is a company that makes big construction trucks and machines. The groundbreaking is tomorrow. That does not give us much time, Tareq. Thank goodness you were there. My mom had mentioned it but I didn't know Ramsey was going to be there."

"You are pleased," Tareq said.

"Not pleased with what is happening, but very pleased that I know more than I knew. Thanks to you."

Up ahead Maggie saw where Oum had set up shop. On the left was a fruit vender whose table was covered with bunches of green and yellow bananas. On Oum's other side were four crates of birds, as well as her green-eyed calico cat. She had been reading the morning paper, which she put down as soon as Maggie got near. Oum cupped Maggie's chin in her hand and kissed her on the top of her head.

Hassan began poking his fingers into the wooden pigeon crate. Alarmed, the birds flapped their wings and shook the dust from their feathers. Hassan laughed.

Maggie briefed Oum on the events of the day before. The only part she left out was the surge of heat that overcame her whole body just before the earthquake.

"So, my daughter," Oum began. "You say that this child was hiding from his uncle. I say that he was waiting for you to pass by. You say the earth shook and disgorged the cats from the temple and tombs of Saqqara. I say Bastet has begun to wake up the sleepy spirits of her legions. The question remains, daughter, what is the connection between the American Ramsey and our children?"

"Exactly. I have a disturbing feeling about this whole thing. The only thing we know is that we have to be ready to act tomorrow."

"Yes," Oum replied. "You must be ready. Come, children. Let us take the boy to a safe place for speaking."

"Where, Grandmother?"

"We shall go to the mosque, Tareq. I will take you to the Al-Mu'ayyad."

"Why not to Al-Azhar, Grandmother? It is there Grandfather prays."

"And that is the reason why not, my son. I want to speak in peace. I would not like to be seen by those whom we know. We have some hours before the noon call. We must go now."

Oum folded up her newspaper and pinned it under the scrap of carpet she used as a seat. Then she asked the banana vendor to watch over her birds while she was gone. The crated pigeons looked on with beady eyes. The green-eyed cat flicked its tail. To Maggie, it seemed like every living thing was wide awake and watchful.

Taking Hassan by the hand, Maggie walked with Oum and Tareq along the busy stretch of Al-Muizz li-Din. They crossed the noisy, crowded intersection of Al-Azhar and continued walking. Maggie almost missed the entrance to the mosque because she was distracted by two gray and black striped cats lounging on either side of a huge wooden door plated with bronze. Like matching pairs of satellite dishes, the cats' large ears stood upright and braced to receive sound. The group turned into the entrance, where Maggie and Oum slipped off their shoes and everyone washed their feet. The cats watched them pass. Continuing through a domed hallway in the direction of the peaceful inner prayer hall, Oum halted. Indicating a square chapel, she pointed to a pair of cenotaphs standing in the depths of the shadows.

"These are the burial places for Al-Mu'ayyad and his son," she said. "For almost six hundred years they have been lying here, and there are always gray striped cats guarding this space. The cats loved Al-Mu'ayyad because he used his brains to plot against tyranny. For this the authorities threw him in a prison that stood here in those days. While in prison Al-Mu'ayyad was plagued by lice. They hopped in his hair and his beard. The lice drove him nearly out of his wits. To get rid of them, he took a sharpened piece of glass and shaved every single hair off his body. Then he vowed that if he should survive, he would build a saintly place on this spot. And so he did."

Lice in an imprisoned hero's beard? Cats as allies? Maggie couldn't get enough of these ancient tales. She hoped she'd be able to remember Oum's stories for *All the Cats of Cairo.* But now she had more urgent things to think about.

Upon entering, Maggie was awed by the spaciousness of the prayer hall. Spangles of morning sunlight shifted along the colorful fringed carpets that covered the entire floor. Smooth carved columns along the length of the room supported massive stone arches. Glass fixtures dangled from the high ceiling, and the blades of wooden fans twirled slowly. Most surprising of all: cats of all shapes and sizes stretched languidly in the patches of sun or sat primly on haunches gazing at the bits of dust held aloft in the streaming rays of light. Maggie was charmed into silence. It occurred to her that she had never seen cats (or dogs, for that matter) in churches back home. The cats of Cairo could go anywhere they wanted. They moved around the city like air.

On the other side of the grand hall, two men in long white *galabiyyas* bowed to the east. Their legs were straight; their hands pressed against their knees. Oum looked at them briefly and kept guiding her small group until they were in an enclosed garden outside the sanctuary. In the speckled shade of palm fronds Oum sat down on a wide smooth stone. Maggie, Tareq, and Hassan did the same.

Maggie invited Hassan into her lap. She put her arms around his small waist and interlaced her fingers. He leaned back and she could smell the way his freshly washed hair mingled with his own scalpy scent. Maggie heard water trickling in a nearby fountain. Oum came closer and listened as the boy, enthroned on Maggie's lap, told his story.

When Hassan finished talking he squiggled off Maggie in order to pet a ginger cat stretched out on a stone five yards away.

"Faithful Muslims know that the cat is a clean animal," Oum said, noticing that Maggie was watching the boy. "The cats are permitted to drink freely of the water bowls in the mosque even before these waters are used for ritual cleansing. Also, my daughter, listen."

Maggie strained her ears. She heard the cat purr under Hassan's stroking hand.

"The purr of the cat has been likened to the *dhikr.*"

"What's the *dhikr*?"

"This is the rhythmic prayerful chanting of the Sufi Muslims. Steady and deep like the purr," Oum said. "The purr connects even the Muslims to Bastet."

Maggie watched Hassan play as Oum translated his experience into English. It all began on an evening not too long ago around dinnertime. His mother was mashing beans. According to the boy, some men had come to his shack near the riverbank in Saqqara. They were wearing traditional *galabiyyas* but they arrived in a big black automobile with darkened windows. While his mother worked the men made an offer. There were nine children in the family, and they wanted only one boy, his brother Barquq. Hassan remembered that his mother wept and moaned for many hours. He could hear her crying whenever he awoke in the night. The next morning when he asked his mother where Barquq was she started to cry again. Nobody would tell Hassan when Barquq was going to come back home.

"Oum?"

"Yes, daughter?"

"Do you think that Hassan's brother is working in Bubastis? I mean, in Zagazig?" It was the first time she had voiced her theory.

"What do you think, daughter?"

"I think yes. But I don't think they're paid enough to save up. I don't think they earn enough to ever get away. And I don't see how Barquq and any other kids like him can ever get away when their families are so poor. But—"

"But what?"

Maggie spoke slowly. She weighed each word.

"Maybe that guard was right. Maybe it's better to work in conditions almost like slavery than to starve in freedom."

"You believe this, Maggie?" Tareq asked.

"Right now I don't know what I believe, Tareq. But I guess that given that Barquq is gone, it's what I want to believe."

Tareq snorted. Maggie felt hurt. Tareq said something to his grandmother in Arabic, and Oum looked genuinely surprised.

"What?" Maggie asked.

"Tareq says he thinks he knows this Barquq. He thinks it is the same boy who was neighbor before earthquake. He asks Hassan if Barquq is missing small finger. The Barquq he knows lost finger when broken window fell on his hand. Before family moved to Saqqara and we came to tomb."

While Tareq slipped over to speak with Hassan, Maggie watched the breeze stir the fronds above their heads. She listened to the trickling water. It is so peaceful here, she thought. No wonder people find comfort in this place.

Tareq came back and she looked straight into his eyes, which were the opposite of peaceful. They smouldered. Obviously, Tareq's suspicions had been confirmed: he knew Barquq. Now what exactly did Tareq expect of her? What exactly did she expect of herself? She tried to put her tumultuous feelings into words. The ginger cat left Hassan and came over to her lap.

"All I know is that Bastet is angry," Maggie said, petting the mosque cat. It rubbed its face hard against her hand.

Tareq shrugged. Oum invited Maggie and Hassan home for a late morning meal and Maggie accepted the offer. She knew Nazaret wouldn't be back at his felucca until late afternoon, and that Tareq would be accompanying Nazaret and the minister on one last trip to Zagazig before tomorrow's event. It would be good for Hassan to take a nap after lunch before the long trip home.

Maggie reached over and laid her hand firmly on Tareq's shoulder. She knew it wasn't customary in Egypt for older girls and boys to touch, but she wanted to get his attention. After his sharp words and the dark look he cast her, Maggie hoped to make peace.

"Tareq, I know you're planning to ride up to Zagazig with Nazaret in a little while. When you're done, will you meet me back at Oum's and come with me and Hassan to Saqqara? Please? I'm sure Hassan's mother will remember you, and then we can tell her that we are going to find Barquq."

Maggie was relieved to see Tareq soften, and even more relieved to hear him say yes.

Oum kissed Maggie on both cheeks. She took Hassan by the hand and Tareq followed them back through the main sanctuary of the mosque toward the front entrance. Maggie let all three of her friends get ahead of her. Walking very slowly with her head discreetly lowered, she stole a glance at the formal motions of prayer enacted by the five men on the other side of the sanctuary. Up and down they bowed. They murmured verses from the *Qur'an*. After completing one cycle they began all over again. It was so formal, so programmed. The other day on the way to the river the formality had bothered her. This morning she saw it as something predictable and comforting.

Maggie took one last look around the beautiful hall. The prayer carpets—knotted wool and silk on grounds of cotton—were well worn from hard use. But the rich colors woven into the textiles—blue, red, green, yellow, sandalwood, white, black—seemed to glow with a warm inviting light. Beautiful geometric patterns bordered each individual rug.

Leaving the silence of the mosque Maggie was struck by an idea. She realized that she would need to clothe herself in something special for tomorrow. Something that would reflect her purpose as *MAU*. But what? What would unite her with Bastet, with the cats, with Aziza, with the all the people of Egypt?

Maggie finally came out the front door to join the others on the busy street. Before going for lunch at Oum's there was something Maggie wanted to do.

"Oum, can you stay with Hassan for a minute?"

"Yes. I wait here," Oum said.

Maggie looked up and down the thoroughfare to see if she could find a place that sold plain cotton *galabiyyas*.

Seeing a shop across the street, she made a dash between the cars and buses. It didn't take her long to try on and buy a simple long white gown. She knew her outfit needed to be white—white like a cloud, like a ship's sail, like the moon-white cat.

"You are sure this is all cotton?" she asked the tradesman, a man with a kind face and a gold front tooth.

"Cotton 100 percent," he said.

"Is it 100 percent Egyptian cotton?"

The vendor looked puzzled.

"I mean, was the cotton in this gown grown here in Egypt?"

The vendor smiled. "Yes. Egypt cotton. Long fibers. Longest in the world. The finest cotton. 100 percent cotton from Egypt."

While Maggie counted out the correct bills, the tradesman folded up the garment and slipped it into a blue plastic bag.

"*Shukran,*" she said as she ran out the door.

"*Ma'as salama,*" he said in reply. "Go in safety."

Chapter 17

Site Unseen

RAMSEY COUGHED in the cement block bunkhouse. "Christ Almighty, the air in here is heavy as Louisiana mud."

The men stood in a narrow, low-roofed, 15 by 30 foot structure. The newly completed building served as the residential quarters for the workers training for Ramsey's Zagazig operation. Right now the workers were fully occupied on the factory floor a quarter mile away, but at night these laborers, boys between seven and thirteen years old, slept on straw-filled mattresses in bunk beds arranged up and down the sides of the cabin. The oldest boys lay stacked in five bunks along the southern and northern walls. The twenty youngest boys slept in a row of cots down the middle of the residence. There was just enough space between the rows of beds for an undernourished body to pass on its way out to work. A small battery-powered fan, suitable for stirring the air in a closet, hummed quietly by the eastern door of the building. In the heat of the day, the silver tin roof quite simply baked the occupants too weak or sick to labor.

Three times a day a lean cook with a long beard delivered two large iron pots to the door of the lodging: one contained either a morning gruel or an afternoon soup; the other held water, which was sometimes enriched with a few cups of goat milk. The children ate and drank out of their own bowls of sunbaked clay, which they were responsible for wiping clean and keeping intact.

Fifty paces to the south of the bunkhouse was a hole in the ground used for a toilet. After delivering the evening meal, the cook sprinkled lime into this pit as a disinfectant.

Once a week, while the children were working in the steamy, cacophonous factory learning to handle dangerously fast-moving machinery, the bearded cook came into the eastern end of the bunkhouse with several buckets of silt-filled water drawn from the Nile's delta. Standing in the open doorway, he splashed this liquid—one bucket after another—all over the floor. Because the residence had been designed with hygiene in mind, the cement floor was graded slightly to the southwest. The fetid, muddy water flowed directly across the length of the dormitory and into a channel leading out a small hole in the southwest corner.

Bill Ramsey was touring the Zagazig site with Delta Cotton's chief engineer, Mustafa Basha, and Minister Mahfouz. At a distance but within hearing, Nazaret and Tareq sat on overturned pails. Several cats lolled nearby. When one approached the Nubian, he scratched it behind the ears and whispered an affectionate word. Nearby, four adult construction workers dug listlessly in a drainage ditch with rusty iron pitchforks. They wore pale blue gowns and long beards; their heads were wrapped in checked scarves. Every so often they looked up to wipe their brows and stare at the wealthy visitors.

Mustafa Basha was a bright-eyed, small-faced man with a tidy little moustache. His low narrow forehead ended like a cliff over deep-set, alert eyes. He had delicate hands and feet, and kept four pens and a tiny calculator in the breast pocket of his white shirt. After attending the Higher Technological Institute in Cairo he had studied engineering in Michigan. Basha kept himself close to Ramsey and continued to murmur words of encouragement in his ear. The engineer wanted to convince the American that he, Basha, was a reliable and forward-thinking Egyptian.

As usual, the trade minister was nattily turned out. The only concession he made to the ferocious sun was a white straw fedora. In his hand he held a long thin cigarette from which blue smoke curled. Around Ramsey he had taken to falling almost utterly silent. By keeping his thoughts to himself, the minister found it easier to manage the revulsion he felt around the American.

The sight of the workers' housing was less than pleasing to the minister, but he folded his impressions of these deprived lives into the overall benefits to be derived from increasing the gross national product. As the westerners liked to say, it was a matter of cost versus benefit. Here the cost was obvious: children were taken off the streets and put to work in conditions nearly indistinguishable from forced labor. But the benefits to children of the future—increased national wealth to channel into housing, schools, education, and medical care: the benefits were unfathomable.

Ramsey had on a pair of hiking boots and a canvas safari hat. With a long walking stick of polished mahogany he poked at the hard-packed earth that crumbled on the end of his stick like baking powder.

"You are tellin' me, Mr. Basha, that you can dig a basement and keep it sealed from this ole river water? I find that hard to believe. If we are goin' to be able to store stock—textiles and machinery and back-up parts—you are going to have to guarantee me a water-tight floor and wall."

In the custom of a negotiating Egyptian, Mr. Basha bowed slightly and put his head very close to his new associate's. Inches away, Ramsey could smell cumin and garlic on the man's breath. Instinctively, Ramsey pulled back until a wider space separated him from Basha.

"I assure you, Mr. Ramsey, this can be done. Our people learned very early how to waterproof the river valley. Our survival depended on this. And the extent of the riches that have been dug up in this delta proves it."

"Give me an example, Mr. Basha." Ramsey pulled a monogrammed cotton handkerchief out of his rear pocket, took off his hat, and mopped his perspiring brow. He dragged the hanky around the back of his neck and swabbed under his square jowls. Then he shoved the wadded hanky back in his rear pocket.

Sitting on the pail, still scratching the golden cat, Nazaret watched and listened. He checked to make sure Tareq was listening, too. Judging by the way Tareq clenched his jaw, Nazaret knew the boy was paying very close attention.

"I will tell you what happened here more than one hundred years ago," Basha said. "This town was built for cotton workers. When the first steam shovels tore into the earth, a vast network of catacombs was revealed."

"Catacombs, sir? Do you mean tombs?"

"I mean catacombs, Mr. Ramsey. But these were the tombs of cats, cats that had been sacrificed and mummified for religious purposes."

"Holy mother of Jesus," Ramsey said.

"Are you familiar with the process of mummification, Mr. Ramsey?"

"No, sir, I cannot say that I studied mummy-making at the University of Virginia."

"The process is a wonder of biochemical engineering, Mr. Ramsey," the engineer said brightly, "whose sole purpose is to avert the effects of deterioration that result from water infiltration."

"Is that so?"

"Indeed. First the body was eviscerated and stuffed with dry earth or sand. Then linen bandages soaked in natron, a preservative, were wrapped around the corpse to cover every square inch. Then these mummified cats were placed in bronze or wooden cases and arranged in the catacombs. There they rested in peace, ever so drily, I might add, until we came through with our earth shovels. By the ton they were dug up, Mr. Ramsey. By the ton. And so dry that people sold the little bundles for use as a fuel source to power trains, much as coal was then used."

Ramsey was enough of a manufacturing man to be impressed.

"If I am understandin' you, Mr. Basha, you are telling me that these old cats were used as fuel."

"Yes, sir. Or at least *sold* as fuel. I'm not sure the world ever in fact witnessed a train running on cat. My American engineering professors would surely have told me that story were it a fact."

"Well, I'll be pinched and baled," Ramsey said. "How about that."

The minister dropped his cigarette on the ground and mashed it out with his toe.

"Gentlemen," he said. "Assuming that Mr. Ramsey is now assured of our abilities to engineer the facility to remain dry in all conditions, I would like to move on to discuss in the presence of both of you the likelihood of beginning work by the end of this week. Mr. Ramsey spoke with me yesterday about urgency in this matter. Madame McKee is likewise hoping to report to her authorities that all parties are in place. Assuming I do what I assured Mr. Ramsey I would take care of, can we all agree that the three of us will meet here with Madame McKee and Mr. Moussa in Mr. Moussa's office tomorrow morning to sign our papers and break ground formally?"

"You can bet your last cotton ball I'll be here," Ramsey exclaimed. For emphasis, the American stabbed the ground with his walking stick. "There's just one little thing I would like to share with you all in confidence."

Ramsey lowered his voice.

"I much admire this here dormitory you have rigged up, Mr. Basha. It seems like just the right sort of place for your young people to learn the benefits of industrious work."

The engineer nodded.

"I just think, gentlemen, that our little Lizzie McKee and her paper-pushing superiors in D.C. might not look as kindly on our efforts, if you catch my meaning. Gainfully employing the fine but extremely *youthful* backbone of Egypt is not something that sits well with my government. American voters outlawed child labor a long time ago. I want your assurance that our ceremonial meeting tomorrow will not bring us into this vicinity but will stay strictly in the area of the proposed construction at the plant proper."

The engineer cleared his throat nervously.

"I take that as an affirmative, Mr. Basha. Now, Minister," Ramsey continued, "can I have your word of honor on this matter today?"

Minister Mahfouz swallowed hard and retained his composure. "Yes, Mr. Ramsey. You have my word."

Nazaret shook his head and looked down at the assembly of cats about his feet. A few of them were holding their heads erect but with eyes closed in meditative dignity.

The meeting broke up and the men parted company. Basha and Ramsey lingered a moment to have a word in private. The minister walked briskly away. Because there was no proper road approaching the dormitory, the two parked vehicles jutted at odd angles on the baked mud near the bunkhouse. Nazaret gestured to Tareq to hold open the rear door for Minister Mahfouz before getting in the front passenger side. They drove off.

Tareq was so angry at the sight of the bunkhouse he leaned against the car door in complete silence. Nazaret studied his employer's face in the rear view mirror. The minister was equally silent. Nazaret spoke slowly.

"Does it seem to your Excellency that Mr. Ramsey's intentions may not suit what our government had in mind for this facility?"

The minister sighed. "Nazaret, the interests here are tangled. My purpose is not to see the individual tangled threads but the whole cloth completed. Before these children arrived here, many had no roof over their heads. And if they did, that roof was most likely on the brink of collapse along with most of the buildings in Cairo. Poor, thin, and hungry, these children are bitter fruits for the picking of extremists, who will use them for civil disobedience at best and for *jihad* at worse. Tareq, I hope you can hear me and understand me. Can you?"

"I think I do, sir."

The minister lit a cigarette.

"Do you remember Farag Fouda, Nazaret?"

"I do, Excellency. The columnist."

"Yes. He was my friend, Nazaret. He was a more faithful Muslim than I by far, and the Islamists murdered him. Why? Because he urged moderation, patience, and humanitarian perspective. But Farag warned us against three feelings that threatened these principles. Three feelings: desperation, disappointment, and frustration. Three feelings. And what happened? Farag was right. Desperation killed moderation. Disappointment killed patience. And frustration killed humanitarian perspective. Together these bitter feelings killed my friend Farag. We must eliminate the causes of these terrible feelings before they kill again."

The minister paused and looked out the window as the dusty date palms slid by along the road south.

"We must find a way to change, Nazaret. We must. Tareq, you hear me now: we must work our way out of bitterness."

Left behind at the site, Ramsey jotted a few notes in his BlackBerry. When he was ready to go, he stuck the gadget in his pocket, spat into the dirt, and called for his escort.

Basha held open the passenger side door of the Range Rover. Ramsey was about to get in when he let out a guttural exclamation that was part surprise, part horror, and part southern obscenity. He reared away from the car as if propelled by an explosion. He fell back into the engineer, who was still holding onto the door handle. The two men lost their balance and nearly toppled over.

"What is it, Mr. Ramsey?"

Ramsey's mouth opened and closed several times like a fish. Speechless, he pointed to the front seat and took another step or two back to make room for Mr. Basha. The engineer craned his neck forward.

Lying upon Ramsey's open briefcase were the bodies of four dead rats. Large black river rats, each one the size of a large melon. Oozing entrails slick with bodily fluids filled the SUV with a sickening stench. Their long hairless tails draped over the rim of the briefcase on all sides; one tail curled over a brass latch. After studying his papers on the trip up to Zagazig, Ramsey had left the briefcase open when he got out of the car. Now all of the folders, papers, graphs, and charts were covered with blood. A head of one of the rats—with sharp yellow teeth harmlessly bared—was lying peacefully upon what had been a neatly typed government document.

"Jesus, Mary, and Joseph, Basha," Ramsey finally blurted. "Who the hell would do a thing like this?"

Ramsey looked up and around, scanning the scene for evidence or witnesses. The minister and his driver were long gone.

What he saw were four local ditch diggers working with their heads down. What he didn't see were the placid faces of nine cats staring at him calmly from the doorway of the bunkhouse.

Chapter 18

Upstream

THE MINUTE TAREQ GOT BACK from Zagazig Maggie woke Hassan from a nap. She was concerned about her promise to Hassan's uncle to get the boy home by sunset. If they took a taxi down to the Nile, they'd have just enough time to boat over to Saqqara and not be late.

In the cab Hassan was still groggy. A sharp left turn tipped him off balance and he stayed put with his head in Maggie's lap. Tareq looked out the window. He had never been in a taxi before.

Maggie put her package down by her feet and rubbed Hassan's back. She had that peculiar feeling again, of being a little family, a little family riding along in a taxi in a big city.

"Tareq, before you tell me about this afternoon, will you tell me what happened to your mother and father?"

"I was four year old when mother die."

Maggie knew better than to correct his mistakes just now.

"How did she die?"

"I was outside playing in alley with big children. Grandfather at coffee house. Grandmother at market. Father sell tee shirts on street. Other brothers with grandmother. Only my mother in our apartment in Boulaq with my baby sister. We live on floor number six." Tareq paused. He looked at Hassan. "Barquq live on floor number three. This one not born yet."

"What happened?"

"It was afternoon. Three on the clock. Older children coming home from school. I playing cowboy. I hold rope and try to swing like lasso. Suddenly ground shake and pieces of building fall on me. Chips of plaster and glass. Very much noise. I curl in a ball and close my eyes. When I open eyes there is smoke and dust and our building has fallen down to the ground. Mother inside."

"I'm so sorry, Tareq."

Tareq paused before continuing.

"After earthquake Muslim leaders come right away to Boulaq to give blankets and food. Egyptian government too slow. Father very sad. Sad and angry. Imam give Father idea and he goes away to find oil work in Saudi Arabia and to study *Qur'an* and to send money. He leave nine years ago. Now I live with grandparents and cousins. Father not come home yet. But some money come month to month."

The boy took a deep breath that seemed to fill his soul with pride and dignity.

"But I will help family. My turn to come."

"You must have felt pretty scared yesterday," Maggie said.

"Not scared yesterday. Not same."

"You mean it wasn't at all the same as that huge one from when you were four?"

"Not same," Tareq repeated. "My grandmother say it was just small warning to remember. Not meant to hurt us again."

Maggie knew what Oum meant. She was sure that yesterday's earthquake had been a warning from Bastet.

"Workhouse at Zagazig," Tareq said, changing the subject. "I feel boys are there, somewhere. You are right, Maggie. And Ramsey show no respect to our Mahfouz. Nazaret knows this but he holds his tongue. Something is not right in the ground. Something is very bad there."

This report was hard for Maggie to follow. It must have been quite a scene up there, with Ramsey trying to make everything work out to suit his own advantage. But it was too complicated for Tareq to explain clearly. Well, soon enough she'd see for herself.

The taxi pulled up to the Corniche el-Nil. The waterfront boulevard was thronged with tourists. Maggie paid the fare and gently roused Hassan, who rubbed his eyes and looked around. They got out of the taxi and crossed the busy street in the direction of the felucca docks. They spotted Nazaret and waved.

Nazaret stopped coiling ropes and greeted Tareq and Maggie.

"Hello, hello! Tareq! Good to see you again so soon! And daughter of Madame McKee! Good to see you again. But today you don't smell of fish. Ha!"

Nazaret clamped Tareq with a hug and then pumped Maggie's free right hand vigorously. Her other hand was holding tight to Hassan's.

"My spirits rise to see you this afternoon," Nazaret said. "Up until now it has not been such a pleasant day, as I am sure this boy has told you. A long silent drive back to Cairo from Zagazig, and the minister in a black mood. But who is this young person?"

Hassan was mesmerized by a gull standing on the dock. Preening his feathers, the gull stopped every few seconds in order to berate a second gull trying to approach. Maggie tightened her grip on the small hand.

"This is Hassan, a friend I made yesterday in Saqqara. We, actually I, was wondering if you might give us a ride from here to there so we can take him back to his mother. I'd pay you, of course."

Maggie looked at Nazaret. "I'm also hoping to talk to you a little bit about Zagazig on the way. Since you and Tareq were just there, I mean."

Nazaret tilted his head back and examined Maggie as if he were studying an interesting rock formation or a rare breed of bird. For thirty years he had piloted tourists up and down the Nile; not one had ever come aboard with a destination in mind. Some people, sick from the congestion of Cairo, came to enjoy the fresh air and open water. Others wanted to be able to say that they'd voyaged on the mighty river. At times a passenger might ask Nazaret to point out the reeds in which Moses had been hidden from Pharoah. Or demand to see the part of the channel through which Cleopatra sailed while charming Marc Antony. But a young American who actually wanted to use the river as his own people had used it for ages, a means of getting from one place to another? This was something new. Something new even as it was something old.

"I can take you where you want to go, my friend," he said. "But you will have to find a taxi or a camel driver to get inland from the river."

"That's okay," Maggie replied. "I know where I'm going. And it's just a few kilometers."

Maggie took hold of Hassan under his shoulders and swung him onto the boat. Nazaret caught him. Then she and Tareq boarded. It was going to be another beautiful evening. Shore to shore, the blue water ran along in a smooth waveless current.

Filled with wind blowing down from the north, the single linen sail of the felucca puffed out like the chest of a pigeon. With tacking unnecessary, there was little work for Nazaret. Once he had pinned the sheet into a metal clasp, all he had to do was hold the tiller steady. The passengers were all arranged in the shade under the white canopy that stretched over the boat deck. Nazaret turned to Maggie.

"What do you want to know that your mother has not already told you, that Tareq has not told you?"

"I have a feeling there is something wrong about this factory," Maggie said. "I have a feeling that there are forces trying to put a stop to what all these people are trying to do. And I know that my mother is unaware of these forces. She's just doing her job. I think everyone's just doing their job, actually."

Nazaret watched her face but said nothing.

"Maybe that's the problem," Maggie continued. "I mean, people just doing their own jobs and not thinking about what doing their jobs means to other people—people, animals, nature, all of everything. And not just the people in the same time. I mean the beings who came before and who will come afterward too. All of *ka.* I don't know. I'm not sure what I mean, actually."

"It sounds like you have been taking Egypt to heart, my friend," the Nubian said.

"I guess so."

"Listen, my young American friend. What happens at Zagazig is nothing that hasn't happened at all times and everywhere. I have nothing to tell you that you do not already know. There is trouble there, as there is trouble everywhere. I could tell you what happened to the land of my people at Aswan. Shall I?"

Maggie wasn't sure what the fate of the Nubians had to do with the events at Bubastis but she knew that the polite thing to do was listen.

"Sure."

"The Nubians descend from the Nubae. We were a large and powerful tribe that emerged from the heart of Africa to rule Ethiopia and eventually southern Egypt. Our kings ruled Upper Nubia, the land of Kush, for generations. To Nubians fell the task of trade. Ivory, gold, obsidian, ebony, spices, Arabic gum, ostrich eggs, feathers, tiger skins, hunting dogs, monkeys, giraffes—all of these and other treasures arrived by caravan from the depths of the continent. Our traders then transported these things downstream to the ports of the Mediterranean Sea. That way."

Nazaret pointed to the north, the opposite direction to the one they were sailing. Maggie nodded.

"But power, my friend, is not what you think. People do not seize power; power seizes people. And power is a wheel, a wheel that rolls where it wants to roll, when it wants to roll. After many years power rolled away from my people. Power rolled through the pharoahs, who quarried our rose granite and carved it into obelisks to commemorate themselves. It rolled through the Persians, the Greeks, the Romans, the Ottomans, and the British. And now power rolls through you Americans."

"And what happened to your people?" Maggie asked, wondering as much as anything what was in store for her country when power rolled away again.

"Our villages were flooded to make way for the Aswan High Dam," Nazaret said. "Today our date palms and waterwheels lie buried under water."

Maggie watched the water ripple by. Nazaret spoke again.

"But something tells me that you have power."

Maggie looked up. How did he know?

"Me?"

"You wouldn't be in this boat if you did not. Neither would this little one. But you must use it wisely."

The rest of the trip was quiet. Nazaret agreed to wait for the children in order to give them a ride back down river. A battered black and white taxi was waiting by the docks. Tareq hired it for the round trip.

Hassan's mother was wrapped head to toe in dark cloth as if in mourning. As she clutched her boy she fell to her knees and praised Allah. Hassan's uncle had obviously terrified her with stories of a white girl kidnapping her precious child. The reappearance of Hassan—particularly in the company of Tareq—was a profound shock. Maggie and Tareq stood awkwardly. When the mother finally lifted her eyes to them, she recognized Tareq and embraced him.

"Can you tell her I want to say something?" Maggie said to Tareq, who was still being fiercely hugged.

Tareq passed along the request.

"Okay," Maggie said. "Now Tareq, please translate this as best you can. It's important."

"I try."

"Tell her I am sorry to have scared her. Also tell her that I am going to try to find Barquq."

Tareq did. Maggie could tell he did because Hassan's mother started to cry and speak in rapid Arabic as she clutched her little boy.

"What is she saying, Tareq?"

Tareq let the woman finish before turning to his friend.

"She says if she ever sees the men who took Barquq away she will slice them open like a fish."

Chapter 19
The Tide Rises

LATER THAT NIGHT Maggie hardly said a word at dinner. Her mother had made couscous with olive oil, garlic, fresh parsley, and lots of chopped tomatoes.

"I have to admit I'm dreading tomorrow," Elizabeth said. "It's been a lousy day, and I don't see why tomorrow should be any different."

"How so?" Paul asked.

"Ramsey has been on everyone's back every single day he's been here. Nagging Shawqi. Nudging the staff. Pushing Moussa and Basha to get things moving. And doing that thing with me that he does, hiding his bossiness and entitlement under a completely aggravating layer of innuendo and flattery and—"

"Whoa!"

Paul tried to placate his wife. Maggie knew how angry her mother was. She felt sorry for her.

"What exactly has he been saying?" Maggie asked, ignoring the signals from her father to change the subject.

Elizabeth turned to her daughter.

"He seems to think there were some fundamentalists at the site today. He thinks they were planted there by somebody inside or outside the Egyptian government to intimidate him. He thinks they were pretending to be ditch diggers but that they were really jihadists or members of the Muslim Brotherhood or something. Evidently Ramsey found a couple of dead rats in his briefcase."

Dead rats! This must have happened after Tareq and Nazaret drove away. Tareq had not mentioned anything about dead rats. Maggie flashed to the pile of dead fish by the embassy on Saturday morning. She was sure that cats had been responsible for those rats. Something fishy had been going on at the embassy, and Ramsey was without a doubt a rat. No message could be clearer.

"But why would anyone want to intimidate him?" she asked. "He's working with the government, right?"

"Yes, but it's all very complicated. Ramsey's been comparing the extremists to the mafia. And he's been going around Cairo from meeting to meeting sounding off about it. He says he's not going to fall for any of these people's scare tactics, and he says no short-sighted Arab nationalist is going to stand in the way of good old American progress, and all kinds of horrible racist stuff like that. I haven't been able to keep a lid on him. And that's what I'm supposed to be doing."

"No wonder you're dreading the ribbon cutting tomorrow," Paul said. "How about if Maggie and I come along on our own?"

"Actually, Dad, I can't make it," Maggie said quickly. Her parents looked at her. "I made some plans with Tareq and

Oum. They're picking me up really, really early—before dawn, actually, and we're going to visit some cousins of theirs who live—"

"That's just as well," Elizabeth said, interrupting Maggie before she could finish making up a fictional day trip. "I'd rather deal with this without you guys. It's gotten too messy."

Paul looked at Maggie suspiciously. But at that moment he was more concerned about his wife than his daughter.

"I'd really like to come with you, Elizabeth," he said, laying his hand on hers. "I promise I won't get in your way. I just want to see all these guys close up. Besides, to tell you the truth, you've got me a little worried and I want to be there in case anything happens."

Elizabeth was too worn out to resist.

"Okay. That's fine if you really want to. I think a car is coming around nine thirty. It's an hour drive more or less and the ceremony's at eleven, right before lunch. Which reminds me: I have to double check that the restaurant in Zagazig is on the ball. We're all supposed to caravan over there after the ceremony for a reception. Baumsdorfer will kill me if that's not totally set up. He even wanted me to ask them to prepare some sort of southern specialty in addition to the Egyptian food. I think he wanted them to do grits, if you can believe it. With Egyptian corn. In honor of the partnership between Ramsey and here."

That night before bed Maggie sat at her desk. Aziza was asleep in her lap. With one hand she stroked the kitten; with the other she twirled her ponytail. After a few minutes of thinking, she decided to phrase it as simply as she could.

Tomorrow we fight back.

An hour before dawn on Tuesday, the town of Zagazig lay shrouded in misty darkness. A tiny white crescent of moon gave hardly any light. The water loving creatures of the delta marshes lay sleeping. South of town, the al-Nasr Qalawun cotton processing facility was still. A backhoe and a dump truck stood in silence against a dark blue horizon. Their large black silhouettes loomed above the flatness of the terrain. Within a square meter of dirt marked off by a yellow plastic sash, a hand shovel was wedged into the hard mud. A few dogs barked, but not a human soul stirred.

Maggie woke up early. Quietly she washed her face and hands and brushed her teeth. Then she put on her white *galabiyya*. The soft Egyptian cotton felt as comfortable as a pair of favorite pajamas. She was glad she had chosen this outfit. If she was going to stand up for Bastet, it was fitting and right that she do so in native cloth whose roots lay in this very land. Maggie buckled on her sandals. She brushed her hair straight and smooth. Fully dressed, Maggie retrieved the figurine and her composition book from under her pillow. She took the long piece of twine she had found in her father's art supply drawer and wound up the figurine. She belted the twine around her waist so that Bastet was pressed against the softest part of her stomach under the gown. She put the composition book in her backpack. Then she plucked Aziza off her bed. The kitten had been sound asleep. Aziza meowed when Maggie wedged her into the backpack. The kitten scrambled around until she could see out. Maggie cinched the opening snug around Aziza's neck to keep her from leaping away.

"Mraugh. *MAU*."

"I know, I know, it's early and this is a weird position. I'm sorry," Maggie whispered. "But you have to come with me this morning. This is a special occasion and we have to do this together."

Passing the kitchen reminded Maggie that she was hungry, but she was too nervous to eat. Instinct told her to put off eating until after the ceremony. She had read somewhere that on very important occasions it was important to fast. It was hard to concentrate on a mission if your thoughts were focused on jelly donuts. Fasting kept the head clear. Besides, there would be time enough for eating later. Maggie slipped out the door and stopped by to greet the hall kittens for the last time. The two kittens were asleep in a pile.

Maggie stood outside on the dark street. She and Tareq had planned to meet in front of her apartment at five forty-five. Together they'd make it to the train station in order to catch the 6:20 up to Zagazig. Maggie looked around. Tareq was right on time.

His eyes widened at the sight of Maggie in her white *galabiyya*. He wasn't used to seeing her in anything but the simple long-sleeved tee shirts and longish skirts she had been wearing since arriving in Cairo. This morning she looked, to him anyway, like a legend come to life. Maggie grinned.

"You like it? Do I look like Egypt incarnate? The idea is to knock their socks off."

"Knock their socks?"

"Hmm. I mean, make them stop and think, but in kind of a dramatic way. Check out Aziza."

Maggie turned and presented her back to Tareq. Aziza's bright eyes peered out from her place in Maggie's backpack.

"Very nice. But we must hurry if we are to make the first train."

Looking out the window as the dismal outskirts of Cairo slid southward, Maggie knew there was something different about Tareq this morning. What was it? She didn't want to stare, but something essential seemed altered. Got it! It was the absence of the musky odor she'd grown accustomed to. This morning Tareq was in clean shorts, a clean tee shirt, and a pair of worn basketball sneakers that he probably borrowed from someone in the neighborhood. She snuck a peak at his hair: it was washed and brushed. Her friend had definitely bathed.

Tareq sat in the aisle seat looking out the window on the opposite side of the train. His hands lay still on either side of his legs, but pent-up energy traveled into his right heel, which was beating a quick and steady rhythm on the train floor. Maggie had a twingy, nervous feeling in the pit of her stomach. She didn't know exactly what was in store this morning, but she was sure that nothing would be the same after today.

The train rattled along for forty miles into the Sharqiyyah province. Zagazig, the capital of the province, had a bustling, if ramshackle, train station. Outside on the curb, five taxis waited for morning passengers. With their morning papers propped on steering wheels, the drivers were all taking in the news of the day. Tareq and Maggie got in the first cab. Tareq told the driver where to go.

"How far away is Bubastis?" Maggie asked.

"Only three kilometers from town," the driver replied, folding up his paper and pulling away from the station. "You visit ruins at Bubastis?"

"Yes."

She reached into her backpack and gave Aziza a little scratch. Tareq reached over and petted the kitten, too.

"Sir?"

"Yes," the driver replied, eyeing his passenger in the rear view mirror.

"Could you point out the main cotton factory to me as we pass? I think it's called the al-Nasr Qalawun. Run by Delta Cotton?"

The taxi halted briefly at an intersection as a minibus huffed by. At eight o'clock in the morning the minibus was crammed with passengers, mostly men on their way to work. Many of them were hanging off the rear fender. As the taxi moved along, the closely built apartment buildings gave way to more slapdash, temporary-looking houses made of tin and concrete. Along the streets Maggie saw old tires, discarded electronics, and rotting garbage. Women carrying buckets emerged from dark doorways to spill dirty water into murky streams that flowed along the curb. After a few more minutes Maggie saw a large low structure off to her right. It was squarish and blocky. The building was surrounded by pavement, the pavement by a chain link fence about ten feet high with barbed wire on top. On the far side of the building the fence was cut and the pavement ran right up to a couple of construction vehicles parked on dirt. Maggie thought she spied a few strips of yellow ribbon and the slanted handle of a shovel.

"There, over there," the driver said.

"Thank you, yes. I see."

Movements ever so slight in the area of the backhoe, slight kaleidoscopic shifts in the colors of the earth around the construction site, told Maggie that others were also beginning to assess the site.

"I'll be back, my friends," she whispered out the window in their direction.

Further along the road past the factory, Maggie and Tareq arrived at the ruins of Bubastis, They stood in silence at the broken remains of the ancient chapel. Maggie got Aziza out of her backpack and held the kitten close to her body. As if materializing from the stones and rubble, thirty cats of all shapes and sizes encircled the visitors. They addressed Maggie.

"MAU."

"MAU."

"MAU."

"MAU."

Aziza pulled herself even closer into Maggie's arm. Maggie smiled and set her gaze upon the cats; she met them each face to face.

"Here I am," she said.

By the dozens the cats continued to approach. Maggie silently met the eyes of each one. Gray eyes. Green eyes. Yellow eyes. Blue eyes. Round and oval eyes. The eyes were sure, the tails held high. Maggie recognized the cats from Heliopolis and the cats who devoured the fish. She saw the mother cat from the hallway—Aziza's mother—and even the calico cat from Oum's poultry stall. One after another, from distances that staggered Maggie to think about, all the cats of Cairo arrived. Eyes wide, they swarmed around Maggie and Tareq. Taking his cues from Maggie, Tareq was neither frightened nor surprised. Entranced, he was suspended in Maggie's mounting power. When the swirl of cats numbered nearly one hundred, and each one had pressed its side along Maggie's legs, they all turned in unison and proceeded to walk in the same direction, deeper into the shadows of the ruin.

"Tareq," Maggie said, "I must follow them. Please meet me back at the factory site at eleven o'clock. If I am not there exactly on time don't worry. I will arrive. Do you understand me?"

Tareq nodded.

"And Tareq?"

"Yes, Maggie?"

"When friends cross paths once, the crossing lasts a lifetime."

Maggie kissed Tareq on the cheek.

Dressed all in white, holding the white kitten, and following a troop of cats that led her away like a living chariot, Maggie seemed otherworldly. Tareq was spellbound. The cats, followed slowly by Maggie, disappeared behind a tall wide column.

After descending a ramp well concealed amidst the ruins of the temple, Maggie found herself in a dark arid chamber. It was practically airless, and she found that she had to take small, shallow breaths just to keep her senses. Aziza mewed quietly. The guiding pack of cats continued walking slowly downward, sure of their destination, surer of their purpose. Shafts of light penetrated through scattered cracks in the ceiling, giving just enough light for Maggie to see, on either side of her, row upon row of shelves. The shelves covered the walls from floor to ceiling. Indeed, the underground cavern was almost like a library, but instead of the shelves being filled with books, Maggie realized that she was looking at the tiny mummified remains of cats. Some of the bodies lay in their linen wrappings. Others were contained in wooden sarcophagi or sheathed in faded strips of papyrus. One cavernous room led to another, which led to another and another. Always following the cats, Maggie passed through six rooms, each one filled top to bottom with cats long dead. In the seventh room the cats paused and arranged themselves in a semi-circle around a fifteen-foot cat carved of stone.

Hewn from the pink granite of Aswan, the Nubian homeland, the stone was three times as big as Maggie herself. In the dim light Maggie could make out the rosy cast of its polished surface. She craned her neck to examine every detail of the shape, design, and expression of the cat. In every respect except size and material, the stone was identical to the figurine Maggie had tied against her own flesh.

The cats lay down and began to purr. The low polyphonic rumbling seemed to soothe Aziza. The kitten finally stopped trembling.

"Bastet," Maggie whispered, hugging Aziza even tighter. Maggie sank to her knees. Tucking Aziza against her cheek, she lay her forehead on the cool paws of the statue. As the stone warmed to her touch, Maggie murmured a prayer for guidance. "Tell me my duty this day, Bastet. I will lie here until I hear your words."

"What the hell is keeping everybody around here? Doesn't punctuality translate into Arabic?"

Bill Ramsey was growing impatient. For more than fifteen minutes he had been standing under the hot sun with a pair of ridiculously oversized plastic scissors in his manicured hand. Every so often he slapped the side of the backhoe whose roof was bedecked in a garland of triangular flags strung on a bright blue rope. Two local musicians had been hired to play at the ceremony. They stood tuning their instruments quietly. A few laborers in dirty pants and loose shirts stood around on bare feet and spoke quietly among themselves. Donkey carts passed on the other side of the fence carrying loads of corn into Zagazig.

"Exactly five minutes ago I was supposed to snip this ribbon, stick this shovel into this godforsaken dirt, and then mount this here rig and make one serious hole—all for the living record. Now why the hell is that not what is happening?"

Nazaret was chatting with a factory official. When Tareq came trotting up the road, Nazaret gave him a big smile. They spoke briefly. Nazaret's eyes widened. Then he nodded.

Paul was sitting on a discarded truck tire sketching the flat delta landscape. He was sure the Living World Books people had no idea what the upper delta looked like. As nervous as he was for Elizabeth, he simply could not resist capturing the images around him.

Her own nerves strung tight as an E string, Elizabeth tried to calm Ramsey.

"I am sorry, Bill, but it's only five past eleven. I'm sure Mr. Basha and Mr. Moussa will be here any minute."

"Lizzie, back home this little scene played out in some podunk backwater of a factory town would have attracted at least one or two reporters from the local rag. And you can bet your last red cent that the local men would be on time, not six minutes, or three minutes, or even two minutes late. Shawqi, where the hell are the real drivers for this doggone equipment? I can't take home a photo of an idle backhoe. I need some smoke, sir. Some action."

The minister flinched. He shifted his weight from one leg to another and looked at Elizabeth. She shot him a desperate plea for forbearance.

"Mr. Ramsey," the minister said, "I do apologize for the delay. It is our pleasure to be able to conjoin the efforts of our two countries. I'm certain I speak for our president himself when I say—"

"Oh, hold the hot air, will you please, sir? It's tropical enough out here as it is."

Elizabeth was horrified. She was just about to chastise him publicly when he spoke again.

"Thank the good Lord, here they come."

Ramsey and the others watched as a black sports utility vehicle pulled up. Paul put away his sketchpad and joined the crowd that now included both employees and locals interested in what these out-of-towners were planning to do. Moussa and Basha emerged from the car. With many greetings and apologies they approached the area of the yellow ribbon. Ramsey glowered but kept quiet.

The speeches began. The minister managed to squeeze out the briefest introduction he'd ever made and slipped back as far as possible from Ramsey. Then Moussa spoke. He thanked the assembled group for their hard work and expressed his hope that it would be the first of many opportunities for collaboration between the people of the Republic of Egypt and the people of the United States of America. Some mild applause followed. Then he held out his arm to Ramsey, indicating that now was the time to snip. Ramsey did so, pausing to grimace at the photographer. The two ends of yellow plastic streamer fluttered to the ground. Ramsey tossed the scissors to Basha. Then the American picked up the hand shovel and stabbed it into the dirt, posing again for posterity. Finally Ramsey marched over to the backhoe. Only then did he smile.

"I see y'all have procured the 710G," he said, laying his large red hand against the massive tread of the shoulder-high wheel. "Not bad. You got a six-cylinder engine on this baby. Y'all oughta make good time at this excavation."

He mounted the driver's seat and seated himself as if on a throne. From behind the glass of the windshield he surveyed the whole area of the construction site, a proud smirk playing on his lips. He nodded to the camera. Then Ramsey turned the ignition key. The engine growled to life and the chassis began to vibrate. Black diesel smoke puffed from the exhaust pipe above the yellow roof. While the digger was in neutral, Ramsey palmed the control knobs. He raised the shovel into the air and cocked its sharp teeth toward the earth. The musicians readied their instruments.

It had been a long time since Ramsey had operated a backhoe, not since a summer construction job during college. The power and strength of the machine ran from the controls up his arms and into his chest. He puffed up with pleasure. Time to put a major pit in the ground and display the might of fully endowed American industry. The shovel jabbed the ashy dirt and hollowed out the first load.

Before the musicians could play a single note, before any of the guests could clap, a low thrumming began. From every direction, the earth seemed to rise toward the work site. A moving tide of brown and gray earth closed in. But it wasn't the earth. It was cats, hundreds and hundreds of cats. Seconds ticked by and it was no longer hundreds of cats; it was thousands of cats. Thousands upon thousands of cats. Cats were streaming to the site from the east, from the west, from the north, from the south. Like a great carpet of fur, a magic carpet sliding along, all of them purring in pulsing unison. The closer they got, the more their voices drowned out the rumble of the backhoe.

A low cry of "oh" spread through the assembled humans as they stared at the flowing ocean of cats. The tide of creatures approached smoothly and ceaselessly.

Elizabeth and Paul watched in awe. The cats filled the spaces of the area with their bodies and climbed up on the fence surrounding the factory. When all the ground was covered, the cats climbed up the fence and perched atop the rail. Thousands of eyes—gray eyes, green eyes, blue eyes, orange eyes; eyes round and oval and almond-shaped; eyes that could see in the dark—all these eyes gazed into the light.

Suddenly there was a rift in the sea as the cats cleaved their solid mass into two halves. From the cordoned off area through the parking lot and out to the west beyond the fence, the cats separated themselves to form an aisle. The aisle snaked toward an opening in the ground through which emerged a figure, still small in the distance. As if on cue, the eyes of the cats turned to gaze upon the approaching figure in white. The deafening purrs grew louder, filling the air with a sound that was almost visible, almost tangible.

Maggie walked slowly forward. Holding Aziza under her left arm, she raised her right hand, palm facing out, and the soul-throbbing purrs ceased.

At first her parents didn't recognize her. Nobody heard Elizabeth whisper her daughter's name.

"Maggie?"

The thousands of cats gave voice to her other name.

"*MAU!*"

It sounded like the earth's own cry.

"*MAU!*"

Maggie walked steadily closer down the aisle created for her by the parting of the cats. She walked on until she stood right in front of the teeth of the rumbling backhoe's shovel. By her feet was the pile of dried silt and mud scooped from the sacred land of Bastet. Maggie picked up a handful of earth, gave it a squeeze, and let it sprinkle out through her open fingers. Then she looked up and faced Ramsey sitting behind glass. His hands lay on the controls. The machine shook with power.

"No more," she shouted over the sound of the engine.

"What the—" Ramsey looked down from his perch at the men surrounding the worksite.

"No more," Maggie repeated.

"*MAU!*"

"Well, I'll be," Ramsey said, his face breaking into a grin. "You're Lizzie here's girl."

"I am MAU. And I say you must not tear apart this land."

"Maggie!" Elizabeth stepped forward. "What are you doing? What's going on? Paul? Maggie!"

"Mag— !" Paul could not utter her name.

Maggie heard nothing her parents said. With the eyes of the cats upon her, she looked up and bored her gaze into Ramsey's eyes. The minister, Nazaret, Basha, Moussa, Tareq, the factory workers and the musicians—everyone—watched her every movement. Maggie seemed to be spellbound, unaware of the fact that a thirteen-ton earthmover could break her with a single touch of Ramsey's hand upon the controls.

Maggie reached out to touch the enormous shovel bucket.

"No!" Elizabeth cried.

"*MAU!*" The cats howled more loudly. "*MAU!*"

"Why, this is ridiculous," Ramsey said, gripping again the red knob of the long-stemmed control. The two sets of backhoe tires, one larger than the other, shifted slightly in their tracks toward Maggie. Maggie did not budge. Aziza hissed at the motion of the gigantic machine. The kitten leaped between two teeth of the shovel. Ramsey swore and gave the shovel a quick jerk upward. Aziza was tossed into the air like a damp rag. She landed on the dirt with a yowl.

Maggie's face was livid. She spoke with power.

"I said NO!"

"Maggie!" Elizabeth cried. "Get out of the way of that thing. There's nothing you can do now. Just get yourself safe and out of the way."

These words seemed to break Maggie's trance. She turned to her mother with a puzzled look on her face. Why was her mother saying these words? What did she mean, there's nothing you can do. Maggie had seen what kind of things happened when people got out of the way. Sometimes a person had to get *in* the way. Now was one of those times. Maggie was sure of it. Bastet was in the way. The cats were in the way. Aziza was in the way. She herself was in the way. And she planned with her whole heart to stay in the way. Maggie reached her arm out, further this time, and touched the hard iron of the backhoe's shovel. She tightened her grip on one of its teeth and held on until her knuckles turned white. She could feel the throbbing tension of the hydraulic force within the machine.

Through the soles of her feet, rising upward in pulsing waves, a searing heat traveled through her blood. Her entire body grew hotter and hotter. She was like living fire, a pillar of fire that was now pumping through her hand, through the extended iron and steel of the backhoe, and reaching up through the machine and into the cabin to scorch Ramsey like a live coal. The expression on his face changed from anger, to surprise, to pain.

"*MAU!*" The cats yowled.

Ramsey cried out. He did not have the strength to get off the burning seat. He did not have the strength to take his hand off the controls. Maggie stood her ground.

Tears streamed down Elizabeth's face.

And then the earth heaved. With an earsplitting roar, the ground began to shift and buckle. One side of the backhoe sank into the dirt and tipped over at a precarious angle. The onlookers, who had until this moment been stunned into a paralyzed silence, began to shout and scream. Across the field, a lightning-bolt-shaped crack slithered down the southern wall of the factory and the roof caved in with a thundering crash.

"Elizabeth!" Paul shouted, grabbing his wife by the arm. "Go! Run! I'll get Maggie!"

Maggie let go of the shovel. Ramsey opened the cabin door of the backhoe and scrambled down to the ground. He fell to his knees as the earthquake siren blared from the center of Zagazig. Then his eyes rolled back and he collapsed. Several officials rushed over to revive him.

Meanwhile, Paul took Maggie firmly by the arm. Maggie turned and shook him off.

"No!"

Maggie wouldn't let her father take her away. She crouched to pick up Aziza and stood up again, tucking the limp and dazed kitten under her chin. Then she felt a strong grip on her other arm. It was Nazaret. He looked more serious than she had ever seen him. Maggie instinctively turned away from her father in order to follow the Nubian. Nazaret guided her back through the sea of cats. They walked past the factory, through a cornfield, and on toward the northern end of the site. Maggie did not know where she was going, but she followed. She followed until they stood in front of the bunkhouse. An angry voice spoke.

"Hey. Stop there! What are you doing?"

Maggie turned and saw Hassan's uncle, the guard from Bubastieion. She recognized him at once by the scratch on his face. The scratch Hassan left when he was trying to get loose. He was holding a ring full of keys.

"You," she said. "You are the one who has been trading the children away, supplying children to Ramsey. Your own family. Your own people."

The guard scowled. "You have never been hungry," he said. " You know nothing."

Maggie looked at Nazaret and moved toward the door of the bunkhouse. She tried to open it, but it was locked. Nazaret shoved his shoulder against the door until it gave way under his strength. Inside, in the stifling darkness, Maggie sensed a crowd of human bodies. As her eyes grew accustomed to the darkness the figures began to move. Maggie turned and led a long file of skinny, sinewy children out of the bunkhouse and into the light. The children were quiet. They looked down as they passed the guard. He said nothing. The cats continued to form a wide purring sea on all sides of the procession.

The minister, Elizabeth, Paul, and the Egyptian officials looked up from the small circle they had made around

Ramsey. They saw Maggie, Nazaret, and the children drawing nearer. The minister looked at Nazaret walking slowly and with dignity. Mahfouz sighed. He wrangled one last time with his conscience before stepping away from Ramsey's side and joining his driver.

"Nazaret," he said, clasping the Nubian's hand. "I suppose we must find another way."

"There is always another way."

"We must let these poor boys go home. Nazaret, take paper and pen and go talk to them. Find where they belong and we can begin to make arrangements for them."

"Yes, Excellency."

The cats' purr crested like a wave.

Elizabeth ran through the cats to her daughter.

"Maggie, where did all these cats come from? And who are all these kids?"

Maggie just looked at her mother. Elizabeth suddenly seemed much smaller than she had ever seemed before. Could her mother honestly not have any idea what was going on here? And if so, what did that say about her?

"Barquq!" It was Tareq, panting from a long run to catch up with Maggie. He recognized his old friend. The two boys clasped each other's shoulders. Maggie watched their embrace and knew that she had done the right thing, even if it had meant destroying what her mother had been working for.

"Maggie," Elizabeth repeated, more urgently. "Maggie! Answer me. Where did these children come from?"

Maggie spoke without taking her eyes off Tareq and Barquq. "Mom, this place was not what you thought. It wasn't a business investment. It was a crime. It has been a crime.

These kids were slave workers. Every one of them taken from their homes to work here for…HIM."

She pointed with disgust at Ramsey. Elizabeth's face fell. Things started adding up. "Maggie, did that little Hassan have anything to do with this?"

"Mom, Hassan's brother is standing right over there. He's the really skinny one hugging my friend Tareq."

Elizabeth watched Maggie's face for signs of further explanations. The minister spoke up.

"Please, Madame McKee. Elizabeth. Your daughter's work here is done. Ours, on the other hand, is just beginning."

Chapter 20

Concerns

Like morning mist under the hot rays of the sun, the vast sea of cats melted away as the emergency sirens blared and police cars sped to the ruined cotton factory. Emergency workers rushed to douse the flames that rose when a gas supply line burst and exploded. Some of the cats would go back to the streets, others to homes in the depths of catacombs long abandoned. Only Aziza remained behind, a small tame white living ball of fur nestled in the folds of Maggie's *galabiyya.*

Maggie sat with her parents by the edge of the cornfield next to the abandoned ceremony site. They were covered with a thin layer of ash and dust. It was high noon. The corn stalks, though fully grown, cast no shadow at all. Her mother held her head in her hands. Her father was watching the frenzied labor of the fire fighters. In a sunken pit, the backhoe lay halfway on its side like a broken toy. Maggie looked at it. It seemed to be a symbol of everything she had been fighting against. Maybe that's why she had felt no fear when she was standing right in front of its powerful shovel. At that moment it was only a big dumb toy about to do something wrong. Maggie was trying to piece together the events of the last few days. What more could she do? And how could she have done anything less? She had stopped Ramsey. That was the right thing to do. There no longer seemed any reason to keep anything from her parents.

"Mom?"

"Hm."

"I'm sorry."

"I'm not sure I understand what are you sorry *for,* Maggie."

"I'm sorry for wrecking your work. I mean, I'm not sorry for wrecking up Ramsey's work, but I am sorry because I know that you were supposed to be helping him... I don't know. I don't know how to explain it."

Maggie looked around. She saw the engineer, Basha, take something from his pocket and deliberately drop it behind his back. It was a fragment of reddish pottery. "So that's who it was," she murmured.

Fully revived and angry as a wasp, Ramsey was deep in conversation with Moussa and Basha. Minister Mahfouz was talking on a cell phone. Nazaret and Tareq were standing with the children they had released from the bunkhouse. Hassan's uncle was nowhere to be seen. Presumably, Nazaret would be getting the information he needed to begin matching each child with his own family. And then what?

"Maggie," her father said, "it would help us if you explained how exactly you came to be here dressed as you are and leading an army of cats."

Maggie took a deep breath.

"I think it began in Heliopolis, Dad. Remember? Last Thursday? I think I started getting the message there. I saw my initials on that obelisk, remember? I told you but you didn't pay any attention. Anyway, from that moment on the cats began to get in touch with me."

Her parents didn't say anything as Maggie went on to tell the story of the last few days. The figurine. Oum. The legends of Bubastis. The encounter between Ramsey and the mystery man that she'd overheard at the museum party.

"Can you tell us a little more about that?" Elizabeth said, raising her head and seeming, to Maggie anyway, to focus on the real story. "Who was that person you heard Ramsey talking to? Who was he making those arrangements with? If I knew that much I could go back to my people and try to get to the bottom of this whole thing. Economic development is one thing. Child labor is something else."

Maggie snorted derisively. "I think you mean slave labor, Mom. Kidnapping and slave labor, to be precise." Maggie let a second pass in silence to let the truth sink in. Then she continued.

"'I'm pretty sure the other person was that guy over there, the engineer. He had the piece of pottery that matched Ramsey's half. I saw him drop it just now. From what I overheard at the museum, I know that the person Ramsey was meeting had a broken piece of pottery that matched Ramsey's to prove his identity. He must have been the one helping to find the kids and get them here. But I'm also pretty sure he had help. Barquq's and Hassan's uncle, for one. He was the guy who stopped me at the Saqqara site the other day. But I'm sure there are others."

"Pretty sure's not good enough," Elizabeth said. "We're going to have to question Ramsey. And the engineer. If Ramsey's been violating international law this will pass out of my hands and into the hands of federal investigators, U. S. and Egyptian. He's going to have to tell us a thing or two about this so-called associate of his. But whether Ramsey goes to prison, pays a fine, or simply leaves Egypt in disgrace is no longer your concern, Maggie. As far as you're concerned, this is over."

"It's not exactly over," Paul said. "I realize that Ramsey is at the heart of your professional problems, Elizabeth. But there seems to be something else of some concern. Our daughter appears to have what has to be called a supernatural connection with cats. Can we please talk about this?"

Maggie couldn't help but smile. She pulled out the Bastet figurine and stroked Aziza. Her parents waited for her to say something.

"How can something be supernatural," Maggie said, "when it all feels very natural. Does this sound crazy?"

Her parents didn't say anything.

"I mean, it's like the cats just needed someone to help them a little bit. And they used me. I was meant to be the person doing this for them. To be doing the parts they couldn't do for themselves. Because they actually did a lot on their own. Like those fish at your office, mom. And the rats on Ramsey's briefcase."

"Well…"

More silence. Now what, Maggie thought. She had no way of knowing what, if anything, she would be called upon to do next. She had no idea what her parents would decide about school, about Cairo, about what she had told them so far. Could her mom really be relocated and sent away from Egypt? All Maggie knew was that thanks to Bastet, from now on, wherever she was she would always be listening. She would be listening for messages. Listening for calls for help. And she would try not to be afraid to respond. Maybe the reason she'd always stuttered was because she'd always been afraid. At least deep down. Afraid to speak her mind. Afraid to be her real self. Supernatural or not, the calls were real if she heard them, and even more real if she responded.

Whether she was in a sacred catacomb in Egypt or a locker room in Washington D.C., she would be paying attention.

Elizabeth got up to speak with Ramsey.

Paul went over to see if there was anything he could do to help Nazaret sort out the needs of the children.

Without disturbing Aziza, Maggie drew her composition book from her backpack. She pulled out *All the Cats of Cairo* and began to make a few notes. She didn't want to forget a single thing.

Tareq came over when she was finished writing.

"Nazaret is taking Barquq home," he said. "What do you do now?"

"I'm not sure. What are you going to do now?"

"I need go back to grandmother. She will be wondering what happened here this day."

"You know, Tareq, I think I'll come along with you. I have to return something that belongs to her." Maggie fingered the figurine. The small black Bastet, now as cool to her touch as a pebble in the shade, lay in her palm. Bastet no longer needed her. The figurine's heat had ebbed for good. Maggie could hardly wait to see Oum and tell her about the great heaving sea of cats—earth, air, fire, and water—all serving a single purpose. "Yes, Tareq, I think I will come with you back to your home. We both need to fill Oum in on what just happened."

"Fill Oum in? I don't understand."

"Let her know what happened. As in 'fill in the blanks.'"

Tareq still looked confused.

"Oh, never mind for now," Maggie said, rising to her feet and brushing off the dust. "Let's just get out of here and back to town. I'm in the mood for a little grilled pigeon."

With a universal sigh, the sacred earth settled into a place of peace for her long buried legions.

All of nature embraced the soothing darkness.

The violators banished, the cat purred pleasure and gratitude into the ears of the girl.

And the girl, awake, gave thanks back.

About the Author

INDA SCHAENEN was born in Dallas but grew up in New York. After college she lived in Paris and Spain, where she taught English as a second language. When she returned to the United States, she worked at various jobs—among them, selling furniture and working behind a deli counter—before she began writing for several newspapers and magazines. Her first book (for adults), *The 7 O'Clock Bedtime,* landed her on the Today Show, and her second book, *Things Are Really Crazy Right Now,* was published in 2005. *All the Cats of Cairo* is her first book for young adults; it combines her interest in the myths and legends of ancient Egypt with the realities of life in Cairo today. If you'd like to write to Inda, her email address is *inda123@earthlink.net.*

Ribbons of the Sun: A Novel

By Harriet Hamilton

In my village we grow flowers. Big, strong, beautiful flowers. Carnations, roses, calla lilies, daisies—all kinds of flowers. When their buds start to open and they are the most beautiful, we take them to Santa María del Sol and sell them in the marketplace. My mother always told me I was her special flower, a gift from la Virgen. That's why she named me Rosa.

Twelve-year-old Rosa begs to go with her father to the city to sell flowers, and when that day finally comes, she can barely contain her excitement.

But her joy turns to despair when she realizes the real reason for her trip to the city—her impoverished family has been forced to sell her into service as a maid.

Assaulted and humiliated by the *patron,* she is thrown out on the hostile city streets to fend for herself. Alone and without hope, her beliefs shattered, Rosa learns to survive and triumph in this emotionally violent but deeply spiritual coming of age story.

A story that will linger in your mind for years.

"the life story of an Indian girl on the threshold of adulthood, cast out by her own people to work in a household that rejects the culture from which she came...an unflinching view of the antagonisms among racially divided groups, yet it conveys the strength of a people who retain their roots." June Nash, social anthropologist, author of Mayan Visions: The Quest for Autonomy in an Age of Globalization

"Hamilton depicts Rosa's indomitable spirit as she eventually reaches into the depths of her spiritual background to recognize her own self-worth. While the story of child exploitation has been told before in other novels, the narrative's simplicity and lack of graphic sexual detail make the book an excellent choice for YA as well as adult fiction collections." *Library Journal,* Sept. 15, 2006

ISBN: 978-09768126-2-3 176 pages $8.95 14 to adult

Brown Barn Books
www.brownbarnbooks.com

KEY TO ATEN

by Lynn Sinclair

Aten? A fantastic world of seductive, bizarre forests and strange deserts, inhabited by fierce clansmen who fight with bows and arrows and all-too-real daggers, violent slave-traders, a magical maze,and mysterious women who live in their own fortress.

The Key? A snake charm 16-year-old Jodi wears the day she touches her sleeping friend's arm—and is plummeted into Aten.

Threatened by the terrors of the alternative world she has unwittingly entered, Jodi also finds love and romance in a handsome young clan leader who may have magical powers. A romantic, exciting novel, the popular choice of teen reading groups throughout the country, a must-have for libraries.

KEY TO ATEN is the first book of the ***Chronicles of Aten*** series, in which Jodi finds she must use the key and her own power, of which she is unaware, to save the alternative world of Aten (and possibly her own) from destruction.

"In *Key to Aten,* Sinclair cleverly combines the elements of fantasy writing—setting the story in an unreal world with incredible characters...—while she explores the very real confusion of the teenage years...This compelling but complicated novel, with its appealing female protagonist, who asserts herself despite the dangers she faces, will attract (those) who enjoy an adventure and acknowledge the uncertainties of adolescence." *Foreword Magazine,* June, 2005.

KEY TO ATEN

ISBN: 9780974648170

12 up $8.95

Brown Barn Books
www.brownbarnbooks.com